All Fathers Are Giants
and Other Stories

All Fathers Are Giants
and Other Stories

Wallace Caminsky

Edited and illustrated by Jeffrey Caminsky

NEW ALEXANDRIA PRESS
LIVONIA

Published by New Alexandria Press
PO Box 530516
Livonia, Michigan 48153
www.newalexandriapress.com

ISBN-10 0-9790106-1-6
ISBN-13 978-0-9790106-1-3

Copyright ©2008 by Wallace Caminsky

Cover design and illustrations by Jeffrey Caminsky.
Cover photo and title photo from Caminsky Family Archives, photographer unknown.

Printed in the United States of America

10 9 8 7 6 5 4 3 2

2007907459

For Alice...and our genes....

Contents

Selected Poems (*cont.*)

Editor's Note

"MAY YOU LIVE IN INTERESTING TIMES," goes the ancient Chinese curse.

As our family's contribution to the "Greatest Generation," my father has seen more of the world—including its joys and sorrows—than he ever realized at the time. Growing up in a poor, Depression-era family, he saw the struggles of hard-working men and women trying to make sense of the wreckage of the American dream. World War II started just as he entered college; and the post-War world showed that saving the world from Hitler and his ilk did not turn it into a warm and fuzzy place: Stalin and the Communists were still a dark cloud on large chunks of Planet Earth, and in his own country, the specter of McCarthyism was casting shadows of its own. Communism took longer to defeat than the Nazis or Imperial Japan, however: the Cold War did not end until the Berlin Wall fell in 1989. And in the meantime, while this country was making progress in some areas, the intolerance shown by Joseph McCarthy and his heirs still infects our public discourse—and has spread to many walks of life, always under the banner of some orthodoxy or other, whether of the Left or the Right.

Dad always read voraciously—both as a little boy growing up on the streets of Hamtramck, and as a grown man—and to this day he still reads everything he can. And he always dreamed of being a writer, studying poets and playwrights, novelists and philosophers, all the while trying to gain some glimmer of understanding into the world around us, and some insight into the human soul. Unfortunately, the demands of the real world always seem to intrude on our dreams, and he seems to have lost his thirst for writing in the 1960s, a decade that broke a lot of hearts across the country; so in his forties, he decided to go to law school—which he did at night, while working full-time for one of the Big Three car companies in Detroit, supporting his family. And he still found the time to come to all of our ball games, music concerts, and awards banquets.

Over the years, Dad amassed a few half-begun novels and novellas, but he also finished a large number of short stories. Some of them, of course, are better than others—but it has been an education for me to see him grow before my eyes, from the tentative and occasionally wordy young man of his youth (whose early work is, nevertheless, touching and brimming with potential) to the mature works he completed in the 1960s. Along the way, he was grappling with the tragedy of losing his father, while savoring the magic of watching his two sons growing up before his eyes. It is a progression that is particularly touching for his eldest son—who has his own dreams of writing, and has followed many of the same twisting and elusive pathways in his pursuit of art, tripping over many of the same roots and branches, and taking pratfalls in many of the very same literary and linguistic swamps.

Dad was always encouraged by his teachers and professors, who saw his potential and sensed the writer he could become. He can be quite funny, as anyone who knows him can attest. His writing can also be touching and quite sensitive—much more so than his son's—and plays on the range of human emotions in ways that elude most of us. Unfortunately, unlike his instructors, the publishers of his day never appreciated what he had to offer, and his work has remained unpublished until now.

Like any editor, I have tweaked things here and there, but his stories remain essentially as he wrote them—the product of a rich imagination, and a love affair with the English Language. As for the raw emotional power he conveys, much of it comes from the richness of his life, and the experiences—from Hamtramck, to the South Pacific, to the post-world of Big Business, the baby boom, and a home in the suburbs—that belong to his particular era. The rest of it comes from the wrenching personal sorrows that sometimes overtake our lives and bring our emotions into sharp focus. All of them are charming, each in a different way; some of them—including the story that lends its title to this collection—are great, and it is a shame that they were never published in the era that spawned them. I did, however, try to preserve each of them within their unique and special time-frame. I also tried to arrange them in an order that would give the reader a sense of growing up in the ethnic neighborhoods of Detroit in the last century...a world now largely lost to suburbs, shopping malls, and video games.

One writer can sometimes envy another's chance to live through adventures that feed the imagination. For myself, though, I can only express my thanks to those who rose from the depths of the Depression to beat back Hitler and Stalin, win the Cold War, and give their children a better, though still imperfect world. Selfishly, however, I'm grateful that my own generation has had less daunting challenges. We are, after all, still busy stumbling our way through them, and making a fine mess of things along the way.

Most of all, though, I'm grateful that my own father was able to hang around, and be there for his sons, grandchildren, and great-grandchildren...sharing life's mysteries and misadventures with us....and that he's finally able to see some of his best work in print.

JC

All Fathers Are Giants
and Other Stories

All Fathers Are Giants

All fathers are giants.
Violent as all giants are,
they tingle with the monumental
whether the monumental be something
Fearful as restitution,
Or exciting as the bleachers,
They tingle.
When the tingle is gone,
Their sons are fathers.

All Fathers Are Giants

SMELLS FROM THE KITCHEN filled the house with the promise of a feast to come. As always, the women fussed and fretted and shooed the intruding men away to where they couldn't steal any of the food before it was ready.

The old man sat in the living room of his son's house, reading a newspaper and watching his youngest grandson play with some toy trucks on the floor. The rest of the family was due to arrive at any time, for dinner was scheduled for four o'clock and it was past that time now. Of course, Sunday dinner was always late, but that didn't bother him. It bothered Alice, his wife, who fretted whenever things were out of place. But it seemed to him that life was full of things out of place, and so he would eat his dinner whenever it was ready.

Suddenly, loud voices filled the house. Julie, his granddaughter, stormed down the hallway in tears, and slammed the bedroom door behind her. Jeffrey, his son, rose angrily from the chair beside him and stormed into the dining room to confront the fifteen-year old boy who was the source of the disturbance.

"Young man, we do not act that way in this family!" Jeffrey stormed, his eyes fierce and menacing.

"She deserved it!"

"We do not say things like that to each other in this house," the father said sharply, glowering at his son. Short but powerfully built,

Jeffrey had been a champion wrestler in his youth, and carried the look of an athlete ready to show no mercy to an opponent as long as victory was in doubt. Combined with a probing, inquisitive mind, his competitive instincts made him an opponent feared and respected in every courtroom in the state. But it was all he could do to hold his own when faced with a rebellious teenager.

"Did you hear– ?"

"Now you go and apologize to your sister. And then you can go sulk all you want until dinner."

"But– "

"Now, young man."

Jason's eyes flared with hurt and anger, but his resolve melted quickly under the furious glare of his father. Grunting rudely, the boy stomped from the room and pounded on his sister's door, mumbling a vague apology that he hoped would be enough to appease the dictators of the house who were always telling him what to do.

Jeffrey watched his son go to make amends, then sighed and visibly relaxed. He returned to his seat beside his own father.

"Sorry. But he's getting to be impossible these days."

"Just take it easy," smiled the old man. "You weren't much better when you were his age, you know."

Jeffrey chuckled and shook his head. A car door slammed in the driveway, and they heard the sound of familiar voices approaching the side door. His father was about to say something else when his eye caught the date at the top of the newspaper.

"Dad...is something wrong?"

The old man felt like he'd just been punched in the stomach. It had been a while since the last time this happened, but it always felt the same. The pain was so vivid and visceral, and the freshness of the memory always amazed him, for it seemed like it was yesterday.

*****

HE MOVED ACROSS the front lawn towards the house. For a few steps, he watched and felt his shoe cushioned by the thick, spongy lawn, then he looked up towards the house and stopped. His mother was on the porch, waiting.

She must have been watching for him, he thought.

The warm light of a passing day in August blurred the line of night and day, and his mother's face wavered between summer and fall.

She was white-haired, round and pretty, standing next to the open front door. Her thick arms were crossed under the flowered apron that her grandson, Jeff, gave her on Mother's Day. Her smile made her face fat-cheeked and round. But the smile looked as if it had been forgotten there; her eyes stared too much.

"Albert, would you close the garage before you come in? Your father forgot." Her voice sounded careful, rehearsed, except for that rising note at the end. The note was jarring and out of place. If he was careful, he thought, he could avoid the rising note at the end and it would go away.

He nodded and walked into the yard, towards the two car garage.

His father had built the garage himself. His parents had only one car, but his father wanted the extra room for the lumber he was always buying. It was a thoroughly competent, professional job, except for the area just below the louvered opening in the peaked roof, where two or three badly fitted planks were pocked with mangled nails and the indentations of a wild hammer. Albert smiled at the bad workmanship, and recalled a day many months before.

He and his family had dropped by for a visit. Pop was at the doctor's for a checkup. But Albert had a sudden itch to do something for his father, and so the bookish son decided to lend a hand on the nearly completed garage. But it had gone badly. And when his father came home and saw just how awful it was, the old man forgot everything in the gigantic rage that followed the discovery.

This is my son, he had roared with arms swinging wide in big Russian gestures. At his first roar, the backyards began filling with neighbors.

My son, he continued rhetorically, who can't even pound a nail straight? The neighbors tittered and got comfortable along the fences.

Next time, he insisted, his voice thick with scorn, it would be better to let little Jeff do it. Some of the neighbors laughed outright and slapped their knees in glee. Then, finding the English language inadequate, his father lapsed into Russian for a final, fiery finish.

Albert flushed and smiled at the memory. Thinking about it now, he decided it must have been pretty funny, but he still wondered how so little of what his father had to teach had rubbed off on him.

He kicked a loose piece of wood into the garage. There was so much lumber stacked on the floor that there was barely room for the car. He pulled down the overhead door and it slammed shut. He looked up at the area under the louvered opening in the peak.

How could it be, he sighed, after living together for so long that the son could mangle a job like that? He shook his head and started towards the house. But for some reason he didn't want to go in just yet, so he lit a cigarette and turned back towards the yard.

It was a comfortable yard, and with the day coming to an end, the fading light made it soft and special. The shrubs along the fence were a virile green, muscling out of the turned black soil. Inside the black frame of the shrub beds, the grass ran smooth to the back of the yard, stopping at the edge of a garden full of radishes, carrots, and tomatoes that grew behind the garage. Albert walked back and pulled up a carrot. The moist earth clung to its flesh, peeling off under his thumb like sunburned skin.

It was a nice yard, he thought. All of it. But best of all was the apple tree. It stood just outside the bedroom window: round and full and straight. Every spring, it covered itself with white pure promises and like a cute little girl seemed to ask: Do you like me? Am I pretty? And every summer, it denied the promises. That was probably why he liked the crazy tree, he smiled. He turned away slowly and walked towards the house, thinking that he would have to do something with his backyard. Maybe an apple tree.

He went in the side door and into the kitchen. There was the smell of supper: beet soup and boiled beef. His mother was waiting for him and he approached her carefully.

"Here's a carrot for you," he said, handing it to her.

*****

HIS MOTHER GREETED him as she always did—smiling brightly, her eyes carrying a look of surprise as though he'd come home from a long journey. But when he bent down to kiss her, she gripped his arm too tightly and returned his kiss too strongly. And when he looked at her, her bright, fat-cheeked smile flickered, then strengthened, then flickered again.

"The carrot was from your garden, Mom," he smiled and sat her down carefully at the kitchen table. He took the seat facing her across the table corner. "Alice called me at work and said something about the doctor. About Pop, she said."

There was a wisp of gray hair on his mother's forehead. She put it in place carefully and seemed for a second to have forgotten he was there. But then she sighed merrily and smiled her bright, fat smile.

"Did you eat?" she asked. "Would you like some beet soup? I could have it warm in a minute."

"No, Mom, no. I'm not at all hungry. I just want to know about the doctor and Pop."

Her fingers played with some crumbs on the table. Albert noticed how the wedding band lay deep and tight about the fleshy finger. He looked at her and she was studying her fingers and shaking her head slowly.

"I don't know," she was saying softly. "I just don't know. But it's something about those pains that he's been having in his side. And today when he saw the doctor, they took some x-rays." Her voice rose sharply on the last word, and she stopped quickly to swallow hard. Albert laid his hand on hers and shushed her calm.

His father called to them from the den.

"Tonia," he called. "Is that Albert?"

"Yes, it is."

"What? I asked you if that was Albert?"

"And I said that it was," his mother returned again in a louder voice.

"Well, tell him to hurry up. Wyatt Earp starts right away."

"Be right there, Pop," Albert called.

"That man and cowboys," his mother complained mildly. "I can't watch anything on TV but cowboys." Frowning, she studied the greasy smudge on the wall over the chair nearest the window. Albert recalled that his father would sit there and occasionally tilt the chair back to lean his head against the wall.

"The x-rays, Mom?" he reminded.

"Something on his right lung," she said in a voice suddenly flat and tired. "Something that has to be checked at the hospital. The doctor said that if he signed in Friday, then maybe they could finish the tests over the weekend and he could come home by Sunday."

"Well, there!" Albert said brightly, spreading his arms wide as though inviting her to share his sunny outlook. "You see? Home by Sunday! So it can't be anything to worry about."

"But maybe it's something serious. Maybe you could phone the doctor? He didn't tell us anything else, but he looked so worried."

"Doctors always look worried, Mom. They take classes in looking worried at college. So don't you worry. I'll talk to him tomorrow after I take Pop to the hospital. But I'm sure it's nothing. It's just that he's sixty-five years old and at that age, you have to be careful.

His mother nodded her head and smiled, agreeing that everything was as he said, that it was silly to worry.

She got up from the table and turned to lead him into the den, then suddenly started. Her husband was standing just inside the doorway to the hall, leaning back against the wall. His left hand rubbed reflectively at his rough stubbled chin. His right arm, permanently bent at the elbow, hung free at his side and looked like a waiter's arm minus the cloth. On his head was a yellow, corduroy hunter's cap that he wore cocked rakishly over one eye. There was a wry, private smile on his lips and an impish gleam in his eye.

"Wasil," his wife gasped. "How you scared me!"

"Lady," he said waggishly, "would you please tell your son that I'm not sixty-five. I'm sixty-four, going on sixty-five."

"Honestly!" she exclaimed. "And his birthday's in two months."

"Listen," he laughed, "two months is two months."

He dragged Albert into the den and told him that Wyatt Earp was in a real fix this week with gun-runners, feuding ranchers and a trigger-happy deputy. Tonia sat down on the studio couch with a magazine.

*****

ALBERT ALWAYS FELT comfortable sitting in his parent's house. He looked at his mother, white-haired and round and pretty, and his father, swarthy and powerfully short. As the sound of gunfire from the television attracted her attention, and she glanced up from her magazine in time to see a body tumble off a high cliff, he heard her say, "When you get back Sunday, let's go for a drive in the country. We haven't gone for a Sunday drive all summer it seems." Then she resumed her story, while his father, absorbed in his show's heroics, gave no indication of having heard her. And it occurred to Albert that the words weren't meant for his father to hear, but were part of an incantation to bring back "Things-as-they're-supposed-to-be." And he understood the need for the magic, for his father and hospitals weren't things that belonged together. Hospitals were for the sick and the hurt. His father was too strong and big and vigorous; nothing could hurt him.

When the commercial came on, his father leaned back in his chair and made a mess of the plastic cover that his mother used to keep the furniture clean and looking new. He swore softly in Russian and tried to fix it.

"Wasil!" the mother exclaimed sharply, a comic look of anger on her face. "Such language!"

"Who but you in this house would understand what I said?" he asked grinning. He stood while his wife bustled about the chair, pulling and tugging its covering back into place. "And why we need that thing on the chair, I don't know," he grumbled gently.

With the cover smooth again, Wasil sat down gingerly, carefully easing himself back. When he was settled again, he wondered aloud whether he had disturbed anything. "Or should I get up again?" he asked with mock concern.

His wife frowned at the quizzical face smirking up at her from under the peak of his yellow cap. With a sudden quick movement, she snatched the cap off his head and held it behind her back, retreating a few steps to block his feigned attempts to retrieve it.

"Why not take off your cap and stay a while?" she asked with heavy sarcasm. He faked a spring from his chair and then leaned back, laughing at her tiny scream and turned to Albert. "You see how hen-pecked I am?" he chuckled. "First, the cover on the seat, then my cap. Next thing you know, she'll make me shave."

Tonia listened with pursed lips. But when her husband turned back and grinned at her, her face went soft and she bent down to kiss him hard on the top of his high, hair-thin forehead. She straightened up quickly and, smoothing down her apron, talked brightly of some tea.

"If I put on the kettle," she asked Albert, "will you have some tea with us at least?

"Why ask?" his father demanded impatiently. "Why ask such a question? If you make it, he will have some."

"Maybe he'd rather have coffee," Tonia said in an exasperated tone. "Maybe?"

"Then you could make him coffee, maybe?" the father

replied with an elaborate shrug. "Or maybe you'd rather have a bottle of beer?" he asked his son.

"Tea would be fine," replied Albert. He laughed at the look of triumph on his mother's face as she left to take care of the tea. Father and son were now alone with Marshal Earp.

Albert saw little of what remained of the adventure. He kept glancing at his father, always having the impression that the older man had just looked away. Several throat-clearings passed, and long breaths that escaped as heavy sighs. Finally, after the Marshal suggested that his viewers try his personal brand of toothpaste, Wasil cleared his throat once more and spoke:

"You will be able to drive me tomorrow?" he asked. "I mean, you won't have trouble at work?"

"No trouble, Pop. I'll be here bright and early."

His father nodded his head and, with the private wry smile on his lips, presently rubbed his chin. It sounded like sandpaper.

"If it's...." he began and stopped and started again. "If it's something you shouldn't do, I don't want you to do it. You shouldn't lose time at work for me." Albert had the impression that he'd started to say something else and changed his mind.

"Come on now!" he protested. "Who's going to argue with my going?"

"Well, just to be sure," his father said. "Just to be sure." He twisted in his chair uncomfortably, messing up the cover once again. Albert grew uncomfortable, waiting for his father to speak and hoping that he wouldn't.

"Your mother," his father started. "Your mother...she worries too much. You should help her, I think. Not to worry, I mean. I mean, if there was something...."

Just then, his mother called to them from the kitchen that the tea was ready. With a relieved look, Wasil jumped to his feet, the plastic cover falling in a heap behind him. "Let's go," he said. "Let's go before it gets cold."

In the kitchen, Tonia was pouring hot water into the teapot. There were some cookies set out on the tray.

"Sit down, sit down," the mother urged. "And try some of these cookies. It's a new recipe that I tried for the first time." Albert's stomach felt empty and the cookie settled like a rock.

"Real fine, Mom. Apple?"

"Apple and coconut."

His father slipped into his seat next to the window. He'd taken one sip of his tea, flinching against the steaming hot, when he almost jumped from his chair. "Hey, I almost forgot," he exclaimed, beckoning Albert with a gesture. "Come on down to the basement. I want to show you something."

"But your tea will get cold," Tonia protested, as the two of them headed toward the basement stairs.

"Right away, lady," said Wasil. "I just want to show Albert something." His slippers slapped each stair as he hurried.

*****

THE WORKBENCH WAS in the corner of the basement to the right of the stairs and under the narrow windows that looked out on the side drive. A supply of nails, nuts and bolts were kept in baby food jars set neatly on the three shelves he'd fastened to the wall over the bench. It reminded Albert of the prescription area in a drug store, with the same neat rhythm and flow of jars.

The tools were all held on a peg board hanging on the wall to the right of the workbench. They'd been arranged with an eye to visual balance as well as utility. A group of hammers here had been balanced by a family of pliers there. A diminishing line of screwdrivers along one edge had its counterpoint in the wrenches along the opposite edge. The tools shone with the loving attention they received even when not in use. The steel gleamed, and the wooden handles had been stained by a strong, sweaty grip until they looked almost like leather. A unique smell filled the area, a pungent combination of hot glue, wet varnish and freshly sawed wood. A layer of sawdust dusted the floor, getting thicker as they neared the saw.

The table saw was to the right of the tool board , separated from the rest of the work area. It was an almost new Crafts-man from Sears. The flat surface around the slit for the saw was powdered with fine sawdust. The dust muted the shine of the saw, and dotted the motor that crouched beneath the table.

Wasil went to the workbench and pressed a switch. Fluorescent lights that he'd installed himself sputtered and lighted. Double tubes of light hung over the saw, lighting it with the promise of Christmases to come. His eyes crinkled with pleasure as he looked at it. He'd finished paying for it the month before and his face was that of a man admiring a treasured heirloom.

"Best thing I ever bought," he glowed. "So many things I can do with it that I couldn't before." He started to demon-strate some of those things when his wife's voice interrupted him.

"Wasil!" she called. "Stop playing with that saw and show Albert what you wanted to show him. Your tea will be like ice."

The father stared at Albert with a comic look of awe on his face.

"How did she know that?"

"Never mind how I know," she called back. "Just hurry up."

"Okay, lady. Okay!"

He went to the workbench. A piece of canvas covered something he'd been working on. He waited until Albert was standing beside him. When satisfied that his son was paying sufficient attention, he removed the cover. He kept his eyes fixed on his son's face.

It was a beautiful, partially completed model of a garage. The skeleton was formed by tiny studs that had been cut individually from larger stock. The wood siding looked like the work of magical little workmen, and the loose planks looked as they'd stacked them there at the close of their day. Minute roof shingles, cut with painstaking care from full size, lay scattered about the base of the garage. Albert squatted so that his eye was level with the base and studied the front of the model. It was an exact miniature, even to the louvered opening in the peaked roof, of the garage in his father's backyard. It was magic, Albert though, like a model train at Christmas.

Something of his wondering delight must have shown in his face, because his father laughed uproariously and slapped him delightedly on the back.

"How do you like that, eh?" he exclaimed. "Jeff will have a garage for his cars even before you."

"Just one thing wrong with it, Pop."

"What's that?" his father asked, bristling.

"You should have let me pound a few of the nails. Then it would have looked exactly like your full-sized garage."

His father laughed and slapped him on the back again. He beamed, then fussed over his work. He sandpapered a bit here, measured a plank that had to be fitted there. And half to himself, half to his son, he criticized his workmanship, noting how he would do it if he could do it all over again. But gradually the delight in his face ebbed and by the time he had replaced the canvas cover, his face had grown wistful.

"There's a lot to do yet," he reflected. "The overhead door, the shingles to finish the roof, more planks, painting. It's too bad I have to go so soon."

"They'll be lots of time, Pop," Albert replied. "When you get back from the hospital. Maybe I could come over and help you. Maybe learn something."

His father snapped off the light and came to his saw and stood there, brushing off the sawdust.

"That would be good," he said, "if you could."

His wife's voice called to them again.

"Wasil and Albert!" she exclaimed. "Will you please come up? And don't bring any sawdust into my kitchen!"

Albert started towards the stairs when his father stopped him. He was smiling at his son a bit sheepishly, and when he spoke, the old man sounded uncomfortable.

"You know all that work we did in your basement?" he asked. They'd partially finished off a recreation area several months before; nothing had been done on it since. "Well, maybe you could finish it sometime, if you had my saw home with you." He stood beside the saw, still brushing at it with his hands, anxiously looking at his son. Then, as though sensing that his face was expressing more than he wanted, his face took on a heavy scowl and in a brusque, bullying tone he added: "Anyone else would have done the job a long time ago. If you had that saw, there'd be no excuse."

"But why give it to me now?"

"So you can finish what we started," the father replied impatiently. "You've got to learn to finish something when you start it. And with the saw— "

"Pop, you know damn well," Albert interrupted, "that I don't know the first thing about using a tool like that."

Wasil's face darkened and he glared at his son. Charging past Albert, he started up the stairs. Half way up, he stopped to glare down at the younger man. He had grown with his anger, and now towered over the son. Big and vigorous and overwhelming with the fierce eyes of an eagle. And Albert felt like a little boy again.

"Well, you could learn!" his father shouted. "You could learn!"

*****

THE OLD HOSPITAL was in a musty part of the city. Young mothers went to the modern hospitals with pastel walls to have their babies. The old people came here.

The three of them checked at the reception desk and were sent down the hall towards the admissions office. The old man broke away from the desk first, walking with angry strides as though trying to leave the others behind. He rolled pugnaciously on his short, bowed legs, his bent right arm held waist high.

Albert half-trotted, trying to keep up with his father while glancing anxiously behind them every once in a while. Trailing by a good distance was the five-year old grandson, Jeff. Absorbed in his inspection of the hospital, the boy walked in lazy pirouettes behind his elders.

"What was he thinking of?" the old man demanded sternly and rhetorically. "What kind of head has he got?"

"For Pete's sakes!" Albert panted. "Will you slow down?"

His father stopped suddenly. Albert slipped past him and had to scramble back. They were in front of the door to the admissions office.

"What kind of place...?" the old man began loudly. The son shushed at him.

"Not so loud," he pleaded. "This is a hospital."

"That's right," his father whispered furiously. "A hospital. And what kind of place is that for a little kid?" He pointed at the boy half-way down the hall, who was tentatively pushing at one of the closed doors. Albert held his father by the shoulders and tried to look into his face. But the old man avoided his eyes.

"Now look—Jeff wanted to come," Albert said earnestly. "And Mom might get even more upset with a little kid around today. You know how she is. Sometimes she worries just to worry. And now—with all this—well, we thought it would be better for her if Alice stayed with her alone."

"Better?" his father scoffed derisively. "Because Jeff wanted it? Who's the father anyway? Better."

"Yes, better!" Albert exclaimed with a sudden burst of anger. He turned a fierce glare at the little boy, verbally prodding him to hurry. The boy started to run with flat-footed, stomping feet.

"You stay close to us, Jeff," Albert warned sternly. "And stay out of trouble, you hear?" He eyed him sharply as though expecting some sign of resistance.

"Don't get mad at him," the old man whispered hoarsely. "Remember, it was your idea."

"Oh, for Pete's sakes! Drop it will you please?"

"Why sure, Albert, sure," his father taunted. "Anything you want. You're the father. I guess you should know best."

Wasil walked away, into the office. Albert stayed in the hall for a moment, his face tight and flushed. The little boy bumped into him. Albert glowered down at him, then breathed a deep sigh and led the boy into the office.

A gray woman with a small, peevish face was at the desk in front of the tall windows that looked out on the hospital courtyard. The nameplate fastened to the file basket read, "Miss Grey." A little woman was in the seat next to the desk. People were in the chairs along one wall, sitting in tight, silent isolation from each other. They looked old, every one of them. Miss Grey looked up from her typing and asked the three newcomers to find seats and wait in the hall. And they did so, except for the boy.

The boy, chunky solid and five years old, stood in the open door, staring at the waiting people. He craned his neck, trying to peer through the open door to the right of Miss Grey's desk. He caught a glimpse of other people on the other side of the door and heard a whirling, clicking sound coming from some sort of big machine that was just beyond his line of sight. After a big round and wandering stare, he caught Miss Grey's eye, and turned all sheepish. He sighed deeply and, clasping his hands behind his back, he examined the ceiling while turning away. His shoelaces were untied.

Miss Grey turned back to her typewriter but watched the little boy suspiciously, the way a bitter, childless aunt keeps a sharp eye on just how close her cousin's children come to the table lamp.

Albert and his father sat stiffly in the two chairs nearest to the admissions office door, looking quite uncomfortable. Jeff squeezed into the space between his father's chair and the empty one next to it and leaned against the wall, watching some men pass and looking down the hall to see that more were on the way. The male patients were taking their afternoon stroll, mostly in pairs, down to the reception desk, where they got their newspapers. They walked with careful, measured steps as though afraid of stepping out of their slippers. When they talked, they talked quietly, adding to the hush of the halls. And when they laughed, it sounded like coughing.

Albert and his father sat without talking for a long time. Abruptly, the old man gruffly asked for a cigarette. Albert hurriedly started to fumble in his pockets, avoiding his father's eyes. Finding a pack, he offered them but, as Wasil reached for them, the younger man seemed struck by a thought and held them back.

"Didn't the doctor say—?" he began.

"He said nothing. Now give me the cigarette."

"Do you really think you should?"

The old man's face darkened with a flush and his mouth took the pained twist of one slightly ill with the taste of swallowed rage.

"Now look, Albert my son," he said in a controlled and carefully measured voice. "I am still your father and I want a cigarette. And no one said I should not have one. And if you don't give me one, I will buy my own—unfiltered!—and I will smoke one right after the other until they are all gone."

Imperially, Wasil held out his hand and waited, a smile twitching at the corners of his mouth, his eyes crinkling with delight. Seeing the suppressed glee in the old man's face, Albert sighed and grinned at him, holding out the pack.

Jeff looked to see two men with listening things hanging around their necks and a girl wearing a stiff white hat come walking down the hall. The boy eyed them seriously. They whispered with a bubble of laughter in their throats, and sometimes the bubble burst into a loud roar. They waved their arms a lot, and their walk was happy and quick like they had someplace nice to go. The rubber on their shoes squished on the cold-looking white floor. It was like a bathroom floor, he thought. Jeff watched them, being careful to wonder in silence. Because it was such a solemn place. Like a bank.

"Sometimes," Wasil said, "you are stubborn, just like your mother." And he leaned back, head against the wall and blew a cloud of smoke towards the ceiling.

"Me, stubborn?" Albert demanded. "You're older than me. You've had more practice." And he lit his own cigarette, puffed on it and then leaned back, head against the wall, blowing a cloud of smoke towards the ceiling. He laid his arm across his father's shoulders briefly and then took it away.

Jeff tugged at his father's sleeve and asked if he could walk down the hall for a drink of water. The fountain was near the reception desk, just past the elevator well. "All right," Albert, agreed, "but don't go wandering off." The boy promised earnestly that he wouldn't wander.

Somewhere on a floor above them, the elevator door opened and closed, and a metallic strum hung in the high, dim corridor. The little boy, attracted by the squeak and rumble, quickened his pace for a closer look. Albert stiffened, alert to the signs of impending mischief. He stood up and called after his son.

"Never mind that now, Jeff. You're going for a drink of water, remember?"

Albert sat back down, still watching the boy who was

dragging himself past the elevators with reluctance, when the old man suddenly chuckled. "You know," he said, "this is only the second time in my life that I had to go to a hospital. The first time was for this arm when I was a boy in the old country." Just above the elbow of his crooked right arm was a deep, raw-looking gouge.

As a boy in the Ukraine, he related, he'd fallen with a heavier boy on top of him and his right arm shattered at the elbow. He had to stay in the hospital for a long time for operations on the arm. One day the doctor came to his bed and showed him a tiny piece of bone and told him he was a lucky boy. If the army ever wanted him, the doctor said, all he had to do was show him his arm and that tiny piece of bone and they'd never take him.

"And you know what I did?" Wasil smiled. "I turned my face into the pillow, held my crooked arm and cried and cried and cried, and told that doctor to leave me alone. He thought I was crazy."

He chuckled a little, squeezing his eyes shut and sighing out the chuckle and shaking his head at the memory.

"Oh, how I cried," he remembered. "Not because of the army or something like that, but because I thought I was a cripple now and not complete or something. Not a boy anymore."

He leaned his head back against the wall once more and stared up at the high ceiling, the small wry smile on his lips. "It's hard to believe sometime," he said, "that I was ever a boy."

Albert started to ask a question, when the elevator door opened and closed. He turned away to look for his son.

The small, broad-backed little boy, hands clasped behind his back, leaned forward to look at the elevator well, then studied the tightened cable and listened to the humming. A shaft of sunlight cast his face in shadow. Beyond him, the corridor ended at a glass through which Albert could see a skinny tree and cars passing on the side street. But the boy's face was a muted phantom in the half-lighted cavern, looking small and tiny in the distance. That was his son, Albert thought, and the echo of the word came back to amaze him.

"The first time," the old man mused, still smiling up at the ceiling, "it was my father who carried me. And now, it's my son and his son who bring me."

"Jeff," the boy's father called. "Jeff, come back, please."

The boy came. Walking backwards. Watching for the elevator. It stopped and a man, wearing a white coat that crinkled and looked like clean clothes smelled, hurried out the door. Running quickly, the man turned the corner.

"Sit down now, son," Albert told him. "We'll be going in for our business soon." He mussed the boy's hair and they exchanged grins. Turning back to the old man he thought for a minute, trying to recall something. Finally remembering, he asked his question.

"How come you never told me that story before?" he asked. "I never knew you'd hurt your arm that way."

"I just didn't think about it too much," his father replied. "You know, it's funny, but lately I've remembered a lot of things about the old country that I didn't before." He hesitated. "Even dream about them," he continued and glanced quickly at the son as though expecting a laugh.

"What kind of dreams, Pop?"

And the old man told him.

He dreamed he was back in his old village. Only he wasn't old like he was now. He was young and strong and straight. His hair was black and curly, and he was amazed to discover that he could bend his right arm again. And everyone there was just the way they had always been—all the young girls, his mother, the boys he'd learned to smoke with, the older brother who died in an accident just before Wasil left for America: everyone. And as he walked down the middle of the dusty village street, they came out of their houses to greet him and walk with him and shout to the houses further down, "Wasil's home! Wasil's home!" And the young girls looked at him like they could never get enough.

He was wearing the blue suit he wore when he left home, but he had nothing in his pockets. No money, nothing. As he had left, so in the dream he came back—with nothing.

And suddenly he was in his mother's house and his mother was standing at the table with the big pot of soup in front of her. She looked at him when he came through the door. His father, a big, strong man, was breaking off a piece of black bread from the long heavy loaf, breaking it across his knee like a stick of wood, and his brother was lifting a spoonful of soup to his mouth. They all stopped and looked at him and shouted his name. And his mother's face squeezed up to cry and she covered her face with one hand and reached for him with the other.

"And then I wake up," the old man said. "Two or three times I have the same dream and I always wake up in the same place. It's so real, I can't remember where I am until I look through the bedroom window and see the apple tree in the backyard. Isn't that something? What does it mean, do you think? That I'm so young and strong and with nothing? And it's so real! That part about my father breaking the bread? I could almost feel those big hands of his, again. You know what I mean?"

But Albert didn't. And he didn't know what to say. He felt guilty, as though he'd read someone else's letter and discovered a secret he shouldn't know.

"I was only eighteen—*eighteen!*—when I left home," his father continued. "And I never learned when my father or mother died, or how."

He thought silently for a long minute, rubbing at his chin that was like sandpaper. It was a while before he spoke again: "You know about my saw? I really think you should take it. I would feel pretty good if you did."

Albert looked away, his eyes searching for his son.

"We'll talk about it later, Pop," he said, still looking away. "This Sunday we can talk about it some more."

Jeff wasn't around any place. Albert stood up, and was starting down the hall towards the elevator to look for him when he heard a woman's voice in the admissions office loudly ask some little boy to leave the room. He hurried into the office at once.

Miss Grey was half out of her chair, leaning across her desk, glaring fiercely at the little boy. Busy investigating the open door to the right of Miss Grey's desk, Jeff did not notice her glowering.

There were lots of people in the room it opened on, most doing nothing but sitting and waiting. But what fascinated the little boy was the shiny machine that whirled and clicked and spit out metal tags when the girl in white touched the keys. It sounded like a robot.

"Sir, really!" Miss Grey exclaimed; an old man with hollow eyes sat at the chair next to her desk. "If this boy is your responsibility, I would appreciate your removing him at once. He ignores me completely."

Albert apologized for his son and, talking a rough hold on the boy's arm, pulled him into the hall. The boy protested against the tight grip and opened his mouth for a louder protest when a threatening, rough whisper from his father closed it into a fat pout.

"Hey, take it easy, take it easy," the grandfather admonished mildly. "He's only a little boy." He grabbed Jeff with his crooked right arm and gently brushed at his hair with the other. The boy leaned back against his grandfather's chest and stared reproachfully at his father.

"Now, don't look at me that way, young man," Albert protested. "It was your own fault for making that lady mad. So will you please stay put and keep out of trouble?"

"Little boys are supposed to get into trouble," the grandfather argued, smiling at his grandson. Then he glanced sharply at his son and added: "But not into old people's troubles."

"Pop, don't start that again."

"I'm not starting anything. But you know I'm right. You ask that lady in there and see what she says."

"Okay, okay. But it's done and we can't change it now. So let's forget it."

"What's done is done," Wasil agreed, smiling his wry smile. "You don't change what's done." Then with his crooked right arm he pulled his grandson closer to him and kissed him on the forehead. The boy objected mildly. The old man hinted to the boy about some surprise he was building for him. The boy's face brightened with excitement, and he begged his grandfather to please, please, please tell him what it was. Oh, but he couldn't do that, the old man insisted. A surprise wasn't a surprise if you knew what it was. The boy would just have to wait until it was done.

Albert rubbed a hand over his flushing face when suddenly Miss Grey called for them. The little boy trotted in first, hurrying to the open door for a closer look at the big, whirling robot of a machine.

The grandfather came next. He carried a hat with sweat stained band in both hands— hard, worn hands—and laid the hat on the edge of Miss Grey's desk. Then he sat down in the chair that Albert had placed for him, rested both hands on top of the desk on either side of the hat, and leaned forward a little. He looked like a man asking for a loan, thought Albert. Frowning down at the old man, he put his hand on Wasil's shoulder and pressed his father back in the chair, gruffly telling him to relax.

Miss Grey briskly rolled an admittance form into her typewriter. The little boy wandered to the windows behind her and gazed down into the courtyard and stared at the windows across. Some patients stood there, looking down at a tiny square of green, blessed by a statue of the Virgin Mary.

Miss Grey asked the old man for his last name. He looked startled and grimaced with the strain of trying to hear words that had already passed. Seeing him cock his head to hear, his son answered for him in a low, thick voice.

"And the first name?"

It was Wasil.

"Middle?"

It was Arcedeff.

And the typing began. Her fingers were quick and firm, and the letters that spelled "Wasil Arcedeff" struck the paper black and irremovable. Or so it seemed to the son. The sight of his father's name printed on the page fascinated him. These letters, printed symbols for exhaled sounds, coming together in this particular combination spelled this one unique meaning: Wasil Arcedeff. This astonished him, and he marveled at the way children are sometimes filled with wonder at the meaning for their names, and explore the sounds for the common denominator of name and self. And this name, they would think, this word was like no other word ever, because no other word spelled Me.

Wasil Arcedeff, Albert read again. And the letters were black.

He shrugged off a sudden chill that touched his shoulder, and found that the flush had left his face. The black letters struck firmly, turning the paper into a page, busy black sounds that hammered a new meaning into place.

Jeff came back from the window and tugged at his sleeve. He picked the boy up and held him until his son protested, gasping, and asked to be let down. He had a question, Jeff said after he'd caught his breath, and it was very important and secret. He whispered into his father's ear.

"Well," Albert suggested, "why don't you wave back?" So the little boy went back to the window and solemnly waved at the man across the courtyard. And the man returned the wave just as solemnly.

Albert watched the unknown man wave while the typewriter in the room continued its black record of occupation, medical history, births, deaths, relatives. He looked down once to help with a date his father couldn't remember, and when he looked up again, the man in the window across the courtyard was gone.

There was suddenly something sweet and precious about the old man sitting in the chair. Albert bent down beside him and, fumbling awkwardly, put an arm around him as though preparing to ward off some blow. The old man looked at him questioningly.

"It's all right," the old man said quietly after a moment. "You shouldn't worry." His look was one of resignation.

Albert got to his feet quickly. He stood, bent slightly at the middle, back and shoulders rounded as though he'd been hit in the stomach. His father's expression reminded him of Jeff's face once at the doctor's, after learning that he had to have a shot. It was the same look of painful resolution, containing the foreknowledge of pain and a little boy's brave resolution to withstand it.

An elevator door down the hall and around the corner slid open and shut. Rubber wheels squealed around the corner, and came down the hall. Jeff hurried to the door, looking towards the father as though expecting some objection, but none came.

Two ladies in white came by, wheeling an old man on a stretcher. Masks hung down around their necks and they looked tired. The man on the stretcher breathed a smell that was sweet and sticky, and his eyes looked funny and loose. There was a silly smile on his face that wasn't a happy one, and he kept trying to snap his fingers but couldn't make it happen. Then he laughed and his laugh sounded like his mouth was full of water.

The little boy stared and flinched against the smell. He backed away from the door until he found his father. He whispered to him, wondering. His father stared at him blankly and didn't seem to understand. And so the boy repeated.

"It was medicine," Albert the father answered vaguely. "Just medicine. To make him all better. That was all it was. Medicine."

There was more the little boy wanted to know. There was more that he needed explained. And he pressed his father for some answers, demanding attention with urgent tugs at his father's coat, whispering daddy-daddy-daddy over and over without any effect. Then finally, he shouted Daddy! and pulled on his father's arm, leaning backwards with all his might, trying to pull his Daddy away from the grandfather's chair.

And the father turned on him fiercely, his eyes like an eagle's glaring. Towering over him, big and vigorous and overwhelming. The boy backed off a few steps, shocked by the rage he'd provoked.

Sit down, the giant commanded, and the little boy sat.

Miss Grey typed in the date and pulled the form from the typewriter. She had the old man sign all the copies, then separated them. She clamped the accounting copies together and handed them to Albert with the reminder that he stop at the cashier's office on his way out.

"And now," she said, "we'll check on the ward. Six bed or ten?"

Albert looked at her a little blankly, his manner gone vague again. "Six, I guess," he replied finally.

She turned her chair to leave and discovered that the little boy had quietly edged next to her and was almost in her lap, his fingers brushing cautiously at the typewriter keys. She coughed and the boy jumped and glanced quickly at his father who was looking elsewhere and didn't notice. The boy backed away.

"Well, we're all done, I guess," Albert said bluffly. He carefully rolled up the forms he held and then unrolled them just as carefully. "Have to drop these off on the way out."

His father looked up at him quizzically and Albert felt himself go hollow. Do you understand now? the look seemed to ask. The eyes asked it gently, emptied of all paternal fierceness. Do you see now? And the son saw a shrunken giant, old and tired and mortal.

In one of the offices across the hall, a phone rang. It rang and rang, and nobody answered it. Then it stopped.

"Everything's going to be all right," Albert said, his voice trembling a little at the end. "You wait and see. It'll be just fine."

His father studied his hands and nodded his head. "Sure," he said, "I know that. Don't worry about it." He called his grandson to him and rumpled his hair when he came. Laughingly, Wasil parried his grandson's questions about the big surprise that was in store for him. Could he have three guesses? the boy begged.

"You couldn't guess with a million guesses," the old man teased. And he let the boy slide off his lap. Wasil rubbed his chin—it sounded like sandpaper—and looked up at his son.

"I'm sure it's going to be all right," he said cautiously as though considering his words carefully, "and I'm not worried. But just in case—you know I am sixty-five years old— "

"Sixty-four going on sixty-five," Albert reminded him with a trembling laugh.

"That's right," the old man smiled. "Sixty-four going on sixty-five. But anyway, just in case, it would make me feel good if you would take the saw." His eyes crinkled. "It's all paid for," he added wryly.

"Sure I'll take it. You bet."

"You know, afterwards I could take it back when every-thing's all right. But for now, you use it. It's easy to learn if you try. For the basement, maybe. Or maybe you can do something on that surprise for you-know-who."

What was it, Jeff pleaded. What was his surprise? Could he know what it was, right now?

"A surprise is a surprise," his father told him. "You don't tell about surprises or it can't be a surprise. When Grandpa comes home Sunday, maybe he'll show you. But don't tease about it. Wait until Sunday."

The boy turned to his grandfather hoping to appeal his father's ruling, but the old man shook his head slowly before Jeff even had the chance.

"What your father says is the law," said Wasil. "So, you have to wait until Sunday." And he looked at his own son, Albert, and gently confirmed the fiction. But there would be no Sundays. The Sundays had been all used up.

Miss Grey came back and announced that there was a bed free in Room 127. Would he go into the waiting room, please? It would be a few minutes. And she indicated the open door where the big machine whirled and clicked like a robot.

The old man got up to go. Albert and the boy made a move to follow. The old man stopped them. "What was the use of waiting?" he asked. "I'm all right, and there is nothing more you can do."

Albert started to protest, but was shut off.

"Don't argue now. I'm still your father. So go home, take care of your family, and you can see me at the visiting hours."

The son nodded his head in agreement, then leaned forward to kiss his father on the cheek. He picked up the boy, who bent his head and allowed his grandfather to kiss his cowlick.

"Bye-bye, Jeff," the grandfather said. "Take care of your Daddy."

"Bye-bye, Grandpa," the little boy said. "I will."

"Say hello to your mother," Wasil said to his son. He hesitated for a second then added, "And take her for a drive this Sunday?"

Albert, the son, promised that he would.

And then his father was gone.

Three Birthdays

MY FATHER, WALTER PETROVSKY, was a dark, fierce-eyed Russian who didn't believe in God.

My mother, Anna Petrovsky, was small and gentle. A Polish-Catholic, she believed in God and prayed to Him often. Every Saturday night, lying next to her fierce husband, she would pray that my father would take her to church the next morning. Sometimes my father would snore loudly and pretend to be asleep. Or, if some anger was burning inside him that night, he would jump to his feet, roaring awful Russian oaths, his arms waving wildly until the rage was spent. Then he would lie down to sleep and let my mother go on with her prayers.

When Sunday morning came, she would put on her black velvet hat with the small rip in the veil, hang her big handbag over her arm and pause at the front door, her gentle eyes hoping that maybe this would be the day.

But Pop would be reading the editorial page of the Sunday newspapers, snorting and sneering at the stupidities he found there. Brusquely, from behind the paper, he would say: "Do not stand there Anna! Go! Your prayers did not work again!"

Sometimes he would put down his paper and look at her when he said it. Then a gentleness would come into his fierce eyes and his angry voice would grow soft. He did, after all, love my mother dearly, and wanted to be tender with her, but there was a principle involved, and when there was a principle, you had to be fierce. (Women never understood this in their men, he later explained to me; they chose to call it stubbornness or pig-headedness or other things that weren't nearly so nice).

But my mother loved her husband as well, and so whether he was gentle or not, she would sigh sadly, and leave him to his paper and his principles. There was always some sort of principle, it seemed. Oddly, though, his principles would change, or maybe just bend a little, with the birth of each new son. In the end, there were three of us.

Joseph:

MY BROTHER JOE was the first. I was ten years old when he left home, but I remember that he looked a lot like Pop. He was quiet and gentle, and he wanted to be a lawyer. He died on a forgotten island in the South Pacific.

When Joe was born, my parents were living with her father in a small town near the Baldwin Locomotive Works in eastern Pennsylvania. The old man owned a small grocery store near the railroad tracks. My father was supposed to be working at the store, but rarely did so because of his political activities. He was an active member of the Socialist Party, and on the night Joe was born, Pop was busy reciting some heroic Russian poetry to a party gathering. It was a matter of principle again. My mother, in the meanwhile, was busy delivering her son with the help of the woman next door—a fat, strong Polish woman who, as an added service, always brought a jar of home-distilled booze for the waiting males. In the days of Prohibition, she was the most popular mid-wife in town.

If not for the police, my grandfather would probably have polished off the jar all by himself. As it was, the town's constabulary raided the Socialist Party Hall just as my father's fervent, impassioned reading was bringing tears to everyone's eyes. This led to a mad scramble for the exits, but since most people were having trouble seeing through their tears, they kept bumping into one another and falling over the wooden chairs, tripping themselves and the police until everything was a confused, cursing tangle on the floor. In all the confusion, my father was actually able to finish reading his poetry—sustaining yet another principle—before making his escape. He ran all the way home, expecting a night stick on the back on his head at any moment.

Stumbling through the store to the living quarters at the back he collapsed, panting, at the kitchen table. His father-in-law, sitting in the chair across the table from him, was glaring red-eyed over the half-filled jar of booze. The old man filled his lungs to speak, forcefully and long, but just as he opened his mouth a freight train came rumbling by. The house shook, the half-filled jar of booze sploshed around, and the old man's torrent of anger at his son-in-law was buried in all the noise. The son-in-law was about to reply in kind (for he had no doubt about what he would have heard...if he could have heard; and he did, after all, have his principles to defend), when the train was suddenly gone, clattering into the darkness, and in the quiet they heard the baby crying.

Maybe it was then, or maybe it was later when he went into the bedroom and saw his young wife lying in her bed in her father's house, nursing their first-born son, that Walter Petrovsky stopped being a socialist. He decided that he didn't want to change the world anymore; he just wanted to find a place in it.

Stanley:

I WAS THE second son. Joe was twelve when I arrived; my mother was thirty-five, and my father was thirty-eight.

The family was now settled in Hamtramck, an enclave surrounded by the big city of Detroit and coming back to life after the bleakest years of the Depression. Factory whistles were blowing again and the men were starting back to work.

It was about this time that my mother began her conversations with God. As a matter of fact, she half-believed that the two of them had come to an agreement about ending the Depression. She was a little puzzled about why He couldn't do anything about her husband's church attendance, but at least she didn't have to go to church alone anymore.

Every Sunday, when the bells sounded from St. Florian's, Joe would escort his mother to the church a couple of blocks away. And a couple times a week—to show that he wasn't taking sides—when the thump of the plants had stopped for a shift change and the factory whistles signaled that it was time, he'd walk down the street in the opposite direction to meet Pop striding home from work, and carry his lunch pail home for him.

My father was working steady now and he contemplated the future with high hopes. He decreed that his next-born child would have the advantages of pre-natal doctor's care and a hospital delivery.

Since I was the next-born child, this was all fine with me. It also added considerably to my status later on, since our neighborhood boasted of very few hospital babies. But for my mother it was a ghastly experience, and one that left her a shaken woman.

She was appalled at how thorough a doctor's examination could be.

"And they looked like such nice, young boys," she would say, shaking her head sadly at the thought of what education could do to a person's morals. Partly because of the doctors, she decided that she would never become pregnant again.

But probably the biggest reason for her new-found interest in family planning was that she just thought it unseemly for a woman over thirty-five to be with child. In her old-country village, people of that age were considered old, and treated with the respect due one of the elders. She concluded that it simply wouldn't look right for her to be pregnant anymore. Though she knew the church might bless the act that caused it, the fact of pregnancy was growing evidence of funny business afoot, and she didn't want people to know that something like that was still going on in her house. But she had problems explaining the nuances of the Church's thinking on the subject to her husband.

"Rhythm!?" he roared. "Rhythm is for the orchestra!" And for a long time after my arrival, my father and his principles were consigned to living a monk-like existence. Maybe that's why he could always terrify me with his rages. Instinctively, like any good Catholic boy, I suspect I always felt guilty.

Ladislaus:

LADDY WAS OUR family's third son. It was 1939; I was seven years old when he was born. And my mother still hadn't changed her mind about doctors.

Laddy started making his presence known on the last day of August. It had been a hot day, but also a wistful day, a sad kind of summer's-almost-over day, one that made little boys complain that Labor Day was coming too early this year, and left their fathers to wonder how many more good years they had left, themselves.

A fresh breeze came with the twilight, promising a cool night. But most of the narrow, crowded houses were still stuffy and warm, so the people—one by one—left their dinner tables to relax on the back steps. The women, shapeless and bulky in their big aprons, stood on the porches, wiping thick hands in their dish towels; the men sat on the steps, a garden hose in hand, religiously wetting down the gently tended green of their tiny backyards. One or two radios were on. There was some trouble about Danzig, it seemed, and people thought there might be news.

Mostly it was quiet. The old country people whispered in their own special language, their round and early Polish sound rising like sad and gentle murmurs. The murmurs all stopped whenever the music on the radio came to an end, but resumed when everyone realized it was just a commercial.

The breeze that evening came from the darker part of the sky. It soothed the trees that crowded into corners between fence and garage, shading the trash cans and sending their roots deep under the alleys.

I was sitting next to my brother Joe on the back steps, listening to the rustling leaves. It made me think of the smoke that hurt when it touched the eyes, and of fires that made the alley bright, flickering along the whole block. And that made me think of our drives out to the country, where

Pop bought bushels of green tomatoes and red tomatoes and hot peppers and cucumbers and apples. For nights afterwards, the house would be filled with the smell of cooking and canning.

"Will we go to the farm soon, Joe?"

"I don't know. Maybe."

We hadn't done much of anything through the summer. There had been one trip to Belle Isle, and we'd had to come back early then because my mother had gotten sick. And we hadn't gone to see a single Tiger's ball game. Joe was working at the Dodge Plant through the summer, earning money towards his tuition at college, where he was a sophomore, and for some reason my father didn't seem interested in baseball anymore.

"Is Ma sick, Joe?"

"No, Why?"

"Pa's always talking about doctors. Why is he always talking about doctors?"

Joe looked at me for a while and then hugged me around the shoulders.

"Ma's going to have a baby. Pa wants a doctor to make sure she's all right."

"And the hospital?"

"This baby is going to be special like you."

We sat quietly for a long time, not moving. The whispered talk of the neighbors seemed reverent and hushed, like talk in a hospital, or funeral home, or bank.

"Will it be soon, Joe?"

"Pretty soon, I guess."

A radio said something about the Prime Minister of England sending a message to Hitler. During the announcement, everything seemed very still. After it was over, it seemed like the whole city was sighing.

"Will there be a war, Joe?"

Joe was about to answer, when we heard loud voices from the house. We stood up and, through the kitchen door, we saw my mother run into the bathroom and slam the door shut. Then Pop started pounding on the door and roaring her name.

"Pa, what's the matter?" Joe called

Pop burst through the door and stood on the porch, staring wide-eyed and breathing rapidly.

"It's her time!" he yelled. "It's her time and she won't go!"

"What do you mean, Pa?"

For a long moment, he could only manage some half-strangled Russian sounds, and then he blurted out: "By herself, she says! By herself!"

I started blubbering, and then I started to wail. My father slapped his hand against his forehead and rolled his eyes up towards the dark sky.

"We got ourselves enough trouble, little Stanley," he shouted, "without your singing! Go next door and get Mrs. Sielenski. And Joe, you go get the doctor."

I ran next door. Mrs. Sielenski had heard and was already tying on her babushka when I knocked. She was very round and her fingers were like little sausages. "Oy-oy-oy," she whispered as she hurried her hard-to-move body.

The bathroom was next to the kitchen. When I got back with our round and worried neighbor, my father was at the locked door, pleading with his wife.

"Anna," he said gently, "Please don't be foolish. Come out so someone can help you."

He was so gentle and soft in his tone that it frightened me, and I started to wail again. I thought my mother was going to die. Pop glared at me and rolled his eyes up again.

"Anna!" he shouted; and then, remembering, he softened his voice. "Anna, please be a good girl. Mrs. Sielenski is here to help you."

Mrs. Sielenski's sausage-shaped fingers fretted along the corner of her apron.

"Oy-oy-oy!" she sing-songed over and over. "Oy-oy-oy!"

My father raised his arms and slapped them to his sides. Then he glowered at the frazzled neighbor lady.

"'Oy-oy-oy,' I can do myself," he roared. "That's not why I want you."

"Oy-oy-oy!"

I wailed louder. Pop was disgusted with both of us and turned back to the door.

"Please, Anna."

My mother's strained voice came through the door.

"It is too late for that now, Walter. You'll just have to wait."

A police siren sounded. It started on the other side of town, came up Joseph Campau and kept coming closer and closer, swelling bigger and bigger, filling the street, and finally slowing down and dying in front of the house. The front door was thrown open, and it sounded like a crowd was stomping through the house, heading towards the kitchen. It was Joe with a doctor and two policemen. My father grabbed the doctor.

"Help, Anna," he said. "She's having a baby."

"Of course," the doctor said crisply. "That's what I'm here for. Where is she?" Pop indicated the bathroom door with a nod of his head.

"Well, ask her to come out, please, so we can get on with it."

Pop's eyes bugged out, his neck corded up, and two gigantic veins popped out on his forehead. "What the hell you think I'm trying to do!" he bellowed.

"Shall we break down the door, doc?" one of the policemen asked.

"You can't do that, Basil," the other one protested. "You'll scar the kid for life!"

"You are the doctor," Pop yelled. "You tell us what to do."

"Oy-oy-oy!" said Mrs. Sielenski.

The doctor thought that there might be too many people in the house and asked everyone but Mrs. Sielenski and Pop to leave. Joe took me out on the front porch and we sat down on the porch swing. The two policemen chased away the small crowd that had gathered around the squad car, and then they sat on the steps and lit cigarettes.

"What time you got?" Basil the policeman asked Joe.

Joe looked at his wrist watch.

"Eleven-thirty."

"Hope this don't take too long. We get off at midnight."

Joe rocked the swing lightly and tried to settle me down. It took a long time, but he finally did. "Ma is going to be fine," he said. "You'll see."

"I was scared."

"Sure you were. So was Pa. So was I. But the doctor's here now. He'll make sure nothing bad happens."

One by one, the lights in the houses down the block had gone out, but no one was sleeping. All the radios were still on.

"Did you hear the news?" one of the policemen asked Joe.

"No."

"The Germans have their soldiers all along the border. They could move any time now. Unless somebody chickens out, it looks like there's going to be a war."

We waited. The swing squeaked and stopped, squeaked and stopped. Far away, the big Stamping Plant thumped, pumping like a gigantic heart.

I got sleepy. My eyes grew heavy and I felt very tired. I must have dozed because I didn't hear my father come out on the porch, and only half-heard him when he sat down on the swing.

"It's all right. Mama's all right, that crazy woman. You got a brother. Oy, that crazy woman of mine."

My father picked me up and carried me into the house.

"Look, Stanley—look!"

With great effort, I opened my eyes and looked. There was Mrs.. Sielenski, a fat, round smile straining against the babushka, cradling a bundle in her big arms. The bundle looked like a red monkey and didn't really interest me.

"You were really wonderful, Mrs. Sielenski," the doctor said in kinder voice than he'd used before. And Mrs. Sielenski's head bobbed with pleasure and her smile spread even further. She walked off with the baby into the bedroom and left him there with my mother.

My father was still carrying me as he walked out with the doctor. The two policemen were still there.

"What time is it , doc?" asked Basil.

"Twelve-thirty."

"That's not too bad. We'll be home by one."

"How's everything?" the other asked.

"Fine," the doctor answered.

"The lady okay?"

"Uh-huh. And the boy too."

The three of them walked to the squad car and climbed in. Basil, who took the seat behind the wheel, stuck his head out the window before driving away.

"By the way," he called back, "the radio says the Germans have marched across the border." Waving, he pulled away.

It was very dark and there was a chill in the air. The breeze freshened and moaned, going between the houses. Pop carried me back into the house and held me in his arms. His cheek was sandpaper rough, and he smelled of tobacco.

From a long sleepy distance, I heard my father and Joe talking about the war. And I felt my father's arm tremble slightly. Even then, half asleep and seven years old, I knew that the little red monkey would be his last son. Summer was over, and soon the world would begin to die.

Always

ACROSS THE STREET was a field. Across the field was a line of trees, with bushes filling the spaces in between. Another street ran along the side of the corner house. Cars going down this street were often in a hurry, so he could never cross it. He could walk down to the corner and back, but no further without permission. He could also walk up his street to Tommy's house, but he must never go further. Not without telling Mother.

He looked at the wall clock. Tick-tick-tick it went, and each tick made the day different.

"Momma?" His mother sat in a chair under the clock, reading.

"Yes, Malcolm?"

"Will Tommy be home soon?"

"Yes, dear. Very soon."

His mother's voice was soft. It soothed him and made Now a safe and quiet place. Her face was pretty, and her eyes were quiet and she never shouted. When she touched his hand or face, he remembered the touch for a long time after.

He leaned his head against the glass of the front window and studied the field. Three small trees stood in one corner.

In the summer they had been green, but now they were red and round and stood there asking everyone to see how pretty they were.

Black crows flew. Their black shone dully, like cold metal. They scolded with harsh words like the sound of a grating noisemaker. They sat at the top of a big tree. They were heavy with their blackness, a dark shadow left over from the night. The branch bounced. They spread their black wings wide like a bad dream. Heavily, across the changing sky, they went away.

He listened to the clock ticking again. The sky was changing, the part that was day leaking out bit by bit.

"Will I go to school sometime?"

"Of course, dear. To a very nice one. It might not be Tommy's, but I know you'll be happy there."

"But will we still be friends?"

"Always. Nothing can ever change that."

Always. It was a fluttering, hard-to-hold word. Did it mean, "tomorrow"? Or did it mean "now and now and now and now"? The field was "Now," but it wasn't "now and now and now" because each tick made it something different. There had been flowers and tall grass that pulled at him when he walked through and whispered for him to stay. And there had been bits of color that fluttered and danced, and bees that hung in the air and made corners going from flower to flower. There had been the floating lightness that walked with him and took him to the secret part of the field where exploding wings would startle him and make him run. But when he saw the red-and-blue-and-gold feathers he would stop and watch, wondering, while the long-tailed bird swooped into another secret place. Other times, the grasshoppers would walk with him to where a rabbit might bound away into the taller grasses.

But now, the light had grown heavy. The flowers were gone and the grass was stiff and brown. If there were any butter-flies, they were slowed by the heaviness and lost, and the bees all went to where the flowers had gone. There was no place for the rabbit or the red and blue and gold bird to hide, so they hadn't stayed. This was the field—Now. Would the other field ever come back, he wondered. What part of it was always?

"Can I play in the field?"

"Just until Tommy comes home, and then maybe a little while longer with him."

The sun was lower in the sky and his shadow stretched long and thin in back of him. Sometimes, his shadow was long and thin in front of him; sometimes it was very fat and under his feet, and sometimes it would not stay with him but would go away.

The field wasn't soft, but crackly like cereal and it pinched at his legs. The tree and bushes at the edge of the field had lost some leaves, and the branches showed and they were dark and crooked. He couldn't before, but now he could see cars passing on the busy highway near the park.

Under the three small trees, there was a log that he and Tommy had found. They had built a strong fort of branches around it. They could be safe behind it, they thought. Nothing could ever break it down. But when the leaves fell off the branches, holes were left in their wall and it would shake, sometimes, when the wind was strong. He sat down on the log and could feel the rough bark without touching it; he ran his fingers across the roughness, testing the gripping grooves and the roundness. It felt just like a tree, but it wasn't because it wasn't holding the ground like a tree would.

He picked up a brown leaf. It crumbled in his hands, the dust of it falling through his fingers to the ground. He had hardly touched it. Once he had tried to catch a yellow bird that always sang in the kitchen. He had closed his fingers around it and felt how warm it was and how it moved. But then the warm moving stopped and it just lay there and it wouldn't sing, and when he showed it to his mother, she had taken it from him. He was a very strong boy, she had said softly. He was a very, very strong boy. And he must always be careful with anything that was small. His friends would all be smaller than he, so he must be careful with them. No matter what they did, he must try not to get angry and hurt them, because he could hurt them very badly. Her eyes were soft, and she told him never to hurt anything smaller. He must always remember. And the bird just lay there.

So the leaf had crumbled, but it hadn't been warm and it hadn't moved. It was different and it was gone.

The ground was freckled by the sunlight coming through the trees. A little breeze came and moved the sunlight very gently. There was a butterfly, a white butterfly. Malcolm watched it for a while, then got up to follow it. It moved heavily, not knowing where to go; it changed its mind all the time—lost because it had gone too far.

The black crows sat heavily on a nearby tree. The branch groaned and bent and the black wings spread wide. The crows sounded angry with their *Caw-caw-caw*. It was a black sound, scraping at the day, darkening it. Malcolm hurried back to the safe fort, and sat down, waiting for Tommy. It was time, he thought. Soon, he thought.

After a while, he heard Tommy call his name. He stood up and his smile came, pulling up the corners of his mouth. He waved his hand with his whole arm from the shoulder, waved it again and again, and then stopped suddenly. The smile was still there, but he'd forgotten it.

There was someone with Tommy. Someone Malcolm didn't know. His hand gradually came down and finally joined his other hand behind his back. His smile crumbled bit by bit, and what was left was small, because Tommy had always come home alone.

"Hiya, Malcolm," Tommy said. "This is a friend of mine, practically my best friend in the first grade. His name is Danny."

"H'lo," said Danny, looking up at Malcolm.

Tommy was also smaller than Malcolm, but not as much as he used to be. He was round and his face smiled most of the time and his eyes were busy, light eyes. Danny was dark and thin, and his eyes were dark and he didn't smile. He didn't look as though he wanted to smile very much.

"Malcom is one of my best friends," Tommy said. "He's very strong and his mother makes good cookies and she always gives me some anytime I want them." Tommy grinned at Danny and then he squatted down to inspect an old ant hole and to have a talk. Danny squatted down and picked up a stick to jab at the ant hole. Malcolm remained standing off to one side.

Tommy picked up some sand and let it run through his fingers over the ant hole.

"Don't you wish you were still in kindergarten?" he asked. "Boy, that was fun! You didn't have to work so hard and you didn't have to stay in school all day. Don't you sometimes wish that?"

"No."

The white butterfly came fluttering by again. Malcolm watched and then followed it, but it was still lost.

Tommy picked up another handful of sand.

"In second grade, you learn cursive writing," he said. "I hope we get Mrs. Snyder instead of Mrs. Haley. My brother says Mrs. Haley beats you for any little thing you do wrong. She has a big paddle that's heavy like iron and it has a lot of holes in it to make it hurt more. Do you think you'll like to write cursive?"

"No."

Malcolm's toe touched something and he forgot the butterfly. He looked down. It was something small and grown and still. He squatted down on his haunches to look at it. It was a small rabbit. Its eyes were open. There was a round red hole in the brown fur. There was blood around the hole. Malcolm poked at it with his finger, but it just lay there. What had happened that it hadn't run to hide? He looked up, wondering, and the field was quiet. The windows across the street were filled with the sun. Tommy's mother was looking in the mailbox. The repairman at Mrs. Barclay's house was getting into this truck and leaving. Mrs. Latimer was walking with her little boy.

"My brother has a girl friend in the fourth grade. He plays touch football everyday after school. Do you like football?"

"No."

Malcolm looked down at the rabbit and poked again gently, but it still lay there. It would always lie there now.

"Is that all you can say is no? Why did you come over if that's all you can say?"

"Look," said Malcolm. The two boys looked at him. He walked to where the rabbit was.

"Look," he said and pointed down.

The rabbit brought a gasp from Tommy, but Danny just looked. They squatted down again, and this time Malcolm joined them. Tommy noticed the red hole and pointed to it.

"That's from an arrow, or a bullet, or maybe just a sharp stick," he advised them. Tommy looked at Danny for support of his judgment, but Danny only yawned.

"I think we should give him a funeral," Tommy said. "Maybe whoever did this will feel so bad when they see the grave that they'll never do it again. You dig the grave, Danny, and I'll make the cross."

"No."

"You're making me so mad I don't know what," Tommy complained. "You're always saying no. You think it's fun to hear you always saying no, or something. I didn't act like that at your house. Why don't you do what I want?"

"Because it's kid's stuff."

Tommy and Malcolm scraped out the shallow grave with a stick. Tommy glared at Danny over his shoulder but was very solemn while digging. They all stood with their hands clasped while Tommy said a few words, and then Tommy stuck a stick at the head of the open grave as a marker. But then, no one wanted to touch the dead rabbit to put it in the hole. And they got into a big argument, with Tommy shouting and Danny simply shaking his head.

"Don't come here anymore if that's all you ever will say!" Tommy stormed.

And when Malcolm said, no he didn't want to, please no, Tommy got even angrier.

"You're so dumb, Malcolm. You're so awful dumb. From now on, you're not my friend."

He stomped away into the fort and sat down on the log to sulk. Malcolm followed him anxiously.

"Tommy—," he began.

"You leave me alone! And get out of my fort!"

Danny stood looking at the angry boy over the dead branches of the fort.

"Is this your fort?" he asked, looking at the browned leaves.

"Yes!"

"It doesn't look like a fort."

"Well, it is!" Tommy shouted, glaring.

"It looks like a pile of dead branches."

"Well, it's a fort!" Tommy screamed.

"Why heck, I betcha I can knock it over with one hand."

"Now, you stop that!"

Danny pulled at the branches, the leaves crunched and fell, and the wall toppled. Tommy rushed at the other boy and kicked at him in a rage. He missed him. Danny pushed at him as he tried to recover for another try and knocked him down. Then he ran some yards away and turned around.

"Yah-yah-yah. You and your dumb ol' fort! It's more of that kid stuff and I tore it down with one little finger."

Tommy scrambled to his feet. His eyes were blind with angry tears and his voice shook.

"Shut up, you dumbbell you! You're not my friend any more! I wish you'd never come back here anymore!"

Danny made faces at him as he backed his way across the field. Tommy threw a stick at him. And the tears came harder and he sat down on the log, shaking his head and growling and clenching his teeth. Malcolm sat down beside him.

After a while, he said, "Should I fix up the fort, Tommy?"

"Shut up!"

"Are we still friends, Tommy?"

"Shut up, you dumbbell! That isn't even a fort at all! It's make-believe kid stuff! Just a bunch of dead branches." And he grabbed at the branches and threw them around and kicked at them. The safe fort wasn't safe anymore. It had been changed into a pile of dead wood and leaves.

"Don't, Tommy," Malcolm said. "You shouldn't. Let me fix it."

Tommy had worked himself into a rage and he swung blindly at Malcolm, hitting him in the chest. Malcolm fell back a few steps. And Tommy followed to attack again, sobbing now, hitting him again and again on the chest and shoulders. Malcolm backed off, his arms at his side.

Finally, the smaller boy jumped up and hit the bigger boy on the nose. Malcolm's eyes filled with tears and he felt the warm blood running down his face and tasted it on his lips. He couldn't see and Tommy was still hitting him, so to stop him, Malcolm caught him in a bear hug, pinning his arms to his sides and squeezing him as he struggled and kicked. "Stop Tommy, stop," he said, but Tommy's struggles to get free grew more frantic and Malcolm squeezed harder. Tommy opened his mouth to scream, but only a labored gasp came out, and his eyes were wide and staring. Malcolm let go, and Tommy sat down heavily, painfully gulping for air. After a moment, he tried to lift his arms and wept a groan at the hurt. He sat there crying, hugging his arms.

"Tommy?" Malcolm bent down towards the boy. As he did, Tommy pushed himself back frantically and struggled to his feet, eyeing Malcolm fearfully. He kept backing away until Malcolm took a step towards him; Tommy cried out in fright and turned, running for home.

"Tommy?" Malcolm called. "Please, Tommy?" His call rang out and part of it came back with an echo. It startled the trees and roused the black, flapping wings.

Tommy ran into his house and Malcolm was alone in the field. He heard the crows and heard the black bounce of the branches. The sun was going. It would be dark soon.

He ran home. The thin, indistinct shadow ran before him; it would be going away soon. His mother met him at the door and held him. And she spoke softly and made the trembling stop. She wiped his nose, and her fingers stroking his cheek and his hair made things quiet.

"Tommy got real mad at me. He hit me."

"He's just a little boy. Little boys sometimes forget and do things they don't want to do."

"Is he still my friend?"

"Yes, darling, yes. Tommy is a kind little boy. He just got angry. You'll see, he'll always be your friend." and she held him for along time, whispering "always" to him. Then the phone in the kitchen rang, and she left him at the window to watch for Daddy while she answered it. Always, he thought. Always. The crows cawed. They were always black, he thought, and even when it was too dark to see, they sat there, looking.

His mother was talking to Tommy's mother on the phone, and Malcolm heard her saying she was sorry. He leaned his forehead against the glass and blinked his eyes.

Across the street, the open field was darkening. Across the field, the line of trees with bushes filling in the space between them looked like a dark wall.

Jamie's Sled

TRYING HIS BEST TO BE gentle, Bill Janik was stepping down the stairs as lightly as he could when Jamie, with a quick wiggle, slipped from his father's arms onto the pavement.

"Christ!" Bill blurted, startled. Jamie, having quite forgotten about the throbbing pain in his jaw, was now skipping merrily down a walkway muddied by the thaw of the post-Christmas snow.

Maybe he's all right, Bill thought hopefully. Maybe we won't have to go after all.

The porch light was on, making the front lawn look even lumpier than it did during the day. High up on the peak of the house, the light illuminated the loose asphalt shingle that the builder never quite got around to fixing. From the porch, Alice Janik called out sharply to her husband.

"Bill," she said severely, "stop that clowning around before someone gets hurt!"

Bill's fleshy face grew tight, and an irritated frown closed over his horn-rimmed glasses. He spoke angrily over his shoulder without turning around. "Dammit, who's clowning around?" he protested. "He jumped down all by himself. You think I threw him or something? He feels better, that's all."

Frowning a bit less petulantly, he turned to face his wife. "Maybe we shouldn't even go tonight. Maybe...."

Alice stamped her foot impatiently and let the aluminum storm door slam shut behind her. The tired Christmas wreath, held to the top of the door by two strips of Scotch tape, lost one of its supports with the force of the closing door, and the wreath dangled awkwardly by its one remaining strip.

"Cut it out, now," Alice said sharply. "Just forget—Jesus! Just look at how you're watching him—just look!"

Startled, Bill's feet tangled and he almost tripped as he turned, ready to rescue his son from whatever danger threatened him. Jamie, wearing one of his Christmas presents—his brand new white boots—was standing ankle deep in the mud of the unpaved street. He was near their '47 Ford, which was already covered by layers of muddy sediment; as Bill moved to retrieve him, the boy kicked more mud on the rear fender.

"See here now!" Bill called out bluffly. "Slop up your new boots if you want to, but leave my car alone. Get out of there before you dirty it some more."

Jamie slogged out of the mud, delighted with the way it pulled at his boots. He started to run and tripped over a half buried piece of crating at the edge of the sidewalk, staggering into his father's arms.

"Almost fell flat on your face, eh?" Bill observed grimly. "See? Just remember that and from now on use the sidewalk. We gotta pay for it, so you gotta walk on it."

Alice, on the stoop, called out anxiously.

"Is he all right?"

"Of course he's all right. You worry too much, for Pete's sakes! Just get back in the house and relax."

"Be sure to keep his mouth covered, Bill."

A heavy woolen scarf, fastened at the back by a big safety pin, was wrapped several times around the boy's lower face.

"Come on now, Alice. Get back in the house and close the door. You're letting all the heat out."

Reluctantly, she backed into the house, peering around the sagging wreath as she looked out at them through the storm door.

"Hurry back, please?" she called.

"Sure, sure. We'll probably be back in time for Arthur Godfrey."

Her young, girlish face was troubled and seemed lined with worry. Bill swore softly to himself.

"You worry too much," he called peevishly. "Why do you worry so much?"

She shook her head and bit the lower lip that had started to tremble. Bill looked quickly to Jamie. It made him mad when Alice showed signs of grief, and he really didn't want to be mad.

"And away we go," he said to the boy. "Wave bye-bye."

And the boy raised a mittened hand close to his face and slowly bent his small fingers once or twice towards his mother. She returned the salute, her eyes blinking rapidly and a trembling smile on her face.

"Come on, Champ," Bill said, taking up his son's hand.

Gently, Jamie removed his hand and, with his pompous little-boy's walk, tried to match strides with his father.

"Well, then!" Bill exclaimed scornfully. "Just keep your old hand if that's the way you're going to be." Delighted, Jamie skipped for a few strides before resuming his grownup walk. Bill ran his finger along the edge of the boy's scarf and checked the big safety pin at the back.

"How is it?" he asked. "Too tight, maybe?"

Jamie shook his head and kept it up until he started to stagger. "All right, all right already!" Bill said, steadying him.

Alice was calling after him. When Bill turned around he saw her standing on the stoop, hugging her bare arms against the damp, chilly air. Her shoulders were hunched, and she kicked her saddle shoes together to warm her feet; she looked thin and innocent, Bill thought. Too little, too sweet for the cares of the world.

"Bill!"she called.

"Get back in that house!" Bill roared with an angry sweep of his arm.

"Tell them to be real careful and gentle," she said anxiously. "Did you hear what I said?"

"Bill?"

She's going to get sick with worrying, he thought bitterly. Why does she have to worry so much?

"I will," he answered impatiently, "I will. Now do as I told you."

Backing into the house, she looked wistfully after them through the storm door.

"Look at her, will you!" Bill exclaimed. "She's going to end up with pneumonia or something!" He gestured angrily at her to get into the house and close the door. Her lips were tight, and she shook her head firmly and refused to move.

Bill glared at her for a long minute. Her hair was up in pins and wisps of it stuck out from under the babushka she'd wrapped tightly around it. The dark sweater she wore had stretched a bit, and was starting to look like something handed down by an older sister. She looked very much like a little girl left with a babysitter, staring after the departing grownups and hoping that they would come back for her. Annoyed, Bill shook his head and noisily cleared his throat.

"All right, then," he said gruffly and took up his son's hand again; once more, Jamie gently but firmly separated himself.

"Pardon me!" Bill said, exasperated. "Pardon me, please! I forgot myself for a minute."

They walked in silence for a little while, before Bill glanced back towards the house. The storm door was all steamed up, but he could still see her looking after them through the little circle of glass she had kept clear. He shook his head and cleared his throat.

"Mothers," he began, then stopped to clear his throat again.

"Mothers are sure funny," he said to his son. "They're even funnier than little boys. And lots more trouble, sometimes."

Jamie skipped, stopped to kick a pebble off the sidewalk, and then started skipping again.

"And sillier. You'd think something awful was going to happen, or something. Like going away for a long time, or starting school."

Jamie put his hand up to his cheek, rubbed it gingerly, and held it there for a while as he walked. Quiet now, his face turned towards the houses they passed, studying the Christmas trees as they let their soft light spill out on the rough lawns.

"As long as you're not afraid," Bill continued hurriedly, "what can hurt you? Nothing! And as long as ol' Papa Bill is with you, what's to be afraid of, eh?"

Solemnly, almost with deliberation, Jamie turned to his father with the clear, long look that was the special property of children, too young to know cynicism and doubt. Then just as solemnly, the little boy looked away, serene and sure in the vision of always beautiful Christmas trees glowing in little white houses that were always and everywhere—but sometimes different. Bill had been proud of the brave, little speech of his, but something about his son's clear, guileless look left him feeling less than proud.

What does he see, Bill wondered uneasily, just before stumbling over a raised seam in the pavement. Regaining his balance, he stepped into an ankle deep mud puddle just off the sidewalk. The wet, dirty cold seeped into his loafer. He shivered and grimaced fiercely at Jamie, who was looking up at him inquiringly.

"Your old man pulled a real boo-boo," Bill said gruffly, and looked away quickly. His socks felt noisy and unhealthy, and Bill felt miserable. Inadequate, mean, and damp with self pity. He inspected himself mentally with abrasive delight: a short, round man who wore bad clothes badly, who looked like a burlesque comic and added to the illusion by playing the fool too much—a clerk in the accounting department of a big company, lost in a warehouse of an office with a hundred other guys, who worried about his job, house payments, doctor bills; about whether he should or he shouldn't, about whether his wife was pregnant again, about whether he could or couldn't. He twisted his head convulsively and stared unhappily at the muddy street.

Damn mud and ruts, he thought. Splashing mud over everything, dirtying the house like it was a farm. Blinds the car, covering the windshield so you can't drive it without wiping it every block, almost. When in hell would they pave it?

And when could he afford a new car? Maybe one with windshield washers!

They couldn't see the house anymore, or Alice. And all the way down the block, Christmas wouldn't go away. It stayed with them all the way down the dark, mud-draggled street. It shined out at them from all the windows, sometimes sputtering until someone finally managed to find the bad bulb. It covered the tiny, brand new evergreens that hadn't grown enough to shoulder the strings of red and green they were asked to bear. The season stayed with them all the way down the bare pavement, melting slowly along with the snow man at the end of the block, who was now a small pile of dirty snow mixed with an old straw hat, an old umbrella, and a broken pipe.

"Look at the poor, ol' snow man," Bill said solemnly.

Jamie looked and was sad. He looked at the Merry Christmas on doors, the wreaths, the fat-cheeked Santas. And he was sad because the snow man had to move to another house, somewhere else.

They crossed the muddy alley, up the side of the old, paint peeling shoemaker shop and turned the corner onto the main street.

It was a shock—after the rush of Christmas crowds, the noise of cars, the scratchy sounds of carols—to see the same street quiet and almost deserted. Some people were there: a few around the theater farther down the street, some young kids giggling and pushing each other down the street, a couple hurrying away from the supermarket with their groceries. But somehow the street looked avoided. Except for the young kids—whose horseplay seemed discordant, like laughter at a funeral—everyone seemed uncomfortable and anxious to be gone. Even cars seemed to hurry down the glistening street. It was like the whole town wanted to stay behind locked doors, as if there were some dark shame they wanted to conceal.

The trimmings were still up, the windows decorated with Christmas, the street crossed by strings of lights and a streamer that still bade everyone *A Merry Christmas and A Happy New Year from THE MERCHANTS' ASS'N*. But it all looked muddied and wrinkled, like a drunk sleeping it off in his clothes, too tired and sick to take them off.

Bill shivered, remembering bills that would have to be paid soon, and glared unsympathetically at the pasteboard Santa Claus in the hardware store window. Santa was listing badly, leaning against the shiny, red sled and throwing a threatening shadow over the deserted erector set Ferris Wheel. None of the clerks inside, leaning limply against the counters, seemed to care about the impending accident.

"Ol' Santa's gonna fall flat on his kisser," Bill observed with grim anticipation.

But Jamie didn't answer. His eyes were wide and he was entranced once more by the fading magic of Christmas, of bikes and trains, sleds and Hopalong Cassidy holsters. Everything bright and shiny and new. Where did they come from, these wonderful things? Who thought them up and who made them? He pressed close until his nose, peeking over the edge of the scarf, touched the window. Then he sighed. A deep, quivering sigh.

And Bill was reminded of Christmas morning again. And his eyes pinched as they had then.

How the little guy stopped in shocked delight and awe! Frozen, with one hand up to his face, the web of sleep melted by the glitter of the tree, rising magically from the mass of brightly mysterious packages. And then, how his eyes grew warm and tender as he looked to Mother and Father, smiling his shy, wondering smile, as though they had truly become reverent beings allied with the miracle, instead of the scowling masters of Can't, Don't, and Mustn't.

That was really something, Bill thought. Almost made it worthwhile.

Almost.

He dreamed for a long minute, staring absently at Santa Claus. Then he came to himself and pawed at his wrist for a look at the time. His watch had stopped.

"Gotta get that fixed," he muttered aloud, and searched for a clock to tell him the time. He saw one in the jewelry store window across the street; it told him it was almost seven o'clock.

"Hey, boy!" he exclaimed. "Let's get with it. We got things to do!"

Jamie nodded his head several times quickly. Then, after a few tentative jabs, he pointed with his mitten hand at the window.

"The train?" Bill suggested fearfully. "Good deal! The six-shooters, then? The sled? The—? You mean, the sled?"

Jamie was nodding his head vigorously and making the glass shiver with his left jabs. One of clerks raised his head briefly at the noise, seemed for the moment resolved to do something about it and then, gesturing with disgust, lapsed back into his black dreams.

"For sure, now?" Bill was saying.

Red, red it was! Slick and fast and shiny! Covered by a little dust, maybe. But red, red and impossibly swift!

"But there ain't no snow, Champ. You may have to wait—"

Jamie looked up at his father and shook his head very slowly, his hand making weaker jabs at the window. His eyes looked fragile, sensitive.

Bill threw up his hands in defeat.

"Okay, okay already," he said gently. "I wasn't arguing. I just wanted to make sure."

He took up Jamie's hand, starting to lead him to the door between the hardware store and the shoemaker shop. The boy hung back and pointed, a little uncertainly, at the store window and the red sled.

"Later, old scout," Bill said quietly. "After upstairs, huh?"

Jamie didn't look convinced.

"Didn't I promise, huh? Didn't I, now?"

The boy nodded and allowed himself to be led to the door.

The door was heavy and dark, and it groaned when it opened. The stairs were bare and worn, and creaked loudly. The bannister was splintered and dusty to the touch; the single light bulb was naked and sick and yellow, and the air was stale with old medicine and pain. Everything was sour with age, grim with the warning that this was no place for laughter or light hearts. And the bantering, happy dialogue that Bill had rehearsed to divert Jamie was stuck in a frozen throat, overwhelmed by the gigantic thumping of his heart.

He wanted to run, to hide behind somebody, anybody. He pressed Jamie closer to him, squeezing him until the boy protested and pushed him away.

"Getting touchy or something?" he said, forcing a laugh that echoed uncomfortably under the yellow light.

He remembered the hospital, the night Jamie was born—hearing a woman yell and, thinking it might be Alice, how he'd longed for a place to hide. He felt the same way now. He wanted someplace to hide. So he wouldn't know. So he wouldn't hear.

The hall was dark and deserted, offices emptied of doctors, lawyers, realtors. Just one dim light was shining over the entrance to the dentist's office. And the smell was stronger—of medicine, of pain, of sobs.

Ringing hollow the footsteps took them forward, and Christmas lay buried in the hardware store far beneath them where nothing could bring it back.

If only he doesn't yell, Bill thought.

At the door, Bill faltered with his hand on the knob. He squeezed his son's strong, fat legs through his rough, muddied leggings. Jamie tightened his arm around his father's neck and trembled, waiting for the door to open.

Chimes announced their coming. There were little chairs and bright, little books, big chairs and picture magazines, cheerful paintings and pictures on good natured walls. And someone ominous was stirring in the inner office.

Bill fumbled at the scarf wrapped around Jamie's mouth. Jamie's eyes were dark and unhappy; Bill looked into them just once.

She can take him next time, he thought. This is too much. After a hard day, this is way too much....

JAMIE DIDN'T YELL at all. Not one bit.

After it was over, he whimpered a little behind a handkerchief he kept pressed to his mouth, and he blinked hard several times to clear his eyes, but otherwise he was quiet. Even the dentist said he was unusually brave for such a little boy.

He lay quietly in Bill's arms as they walked down the stairs, his head resting on his father's shoulder, trembling a little and, every once in a while, breathing a heavy, sobbing sigh.

Bill's knees were weak and his stomach was still in knots. The blood on the handkerchief had dazed him. He cooed wordlessly into Jamie's ear, hardly knowing it, and touched his cheek with his lips, the way he used to when Jamie was very little and unable to sleep because of his sore, tender gums.

"Now we get our present and go home to Mommy and Godfrey, eh? Such a brave, little boy. Never has there been such a brave, little boy. I tell you, I'm proud of my brave, little boy. Awful, awful proud."

He could almost taste it: the smell of medicine, the smell of pain—old, dusty pain. He felt better when they got outside again. Even Jamie lifted his head to sniff at the wetness, the mud and mist.

Still cooing and concentrating on Jamie and his hurt, Bill walked to the door of the hardware store. He pushed at it and it didn't open. He pushed a few more times, then stepped back and realized that it *wouldn't* open. The store was closed.

The hardware store was closed.

Closed, he thought. It can't be closed. I've got to get Jamie his sled!

"Jamie," he said faintly. "It's closed. How about that? It's really closed."

The boy had laid his head down on the shoulder again, motionless, making no sound except his heavy, sighing breathing, muffled by the handkerchief.

"I forgot that it closes early now. Forgot all about it, cross my heart."

He walked from the door dazedly and stopped in front of the window. Santa had finally fallen; he lay on his face on top of the remains of the demolished Ferris Wheel, exposing his gray, pasteboard back and prop. Parts of the toy had skidded across the top of the red sled, making long lines in the dust.

Jamie stirred just a little for a look at his fast, shiny sled and was still again.

"What a boo-boo I pulled," Bill fretted. "What a king-sized boo-boo. I should have known they wouldn't be open as long after Christmas. I should have listened to you." He rocked his son gently, as the boy looked wistfully at the bright red sled.

"I'm real, real sorry."

Bill stared at the sled for a long minute, trying to think. Finally, forcing a bright tone, he said: "But I tell you what! You know what? How about if I take you home first, then I'll go right out again and find a sled just like that one for you. Even if I have to go all over the city. How does that sound, eh?"

Bill fumbled with the boy's cap, worried over the muffler coming loose because the safety pin was lost. And he touched the boy's face often. Suddenly, he couldn't get enough of touching the boy's face.

"Is that all right, Jamie?" he pleaded now. "Will it be all right if we do that?"

Jamie nodded. "Sure, Daddy," he said, his voice muffled and faint.

And something inside throbbed and something turned paper thin and crumbled, and Bill couldn't see very well, and he mourned the pain and grief of never fulfilling the expectation in a boy's eyes, the Christmas always followed by the after-Christmas.

"Mommy?" said Jamie.

"You betcha," Bill replied. "You betch'er boots."

He would fail him, Bill thought. One day, he was bound to fail his son. There would be no red sleds, Santa would fall flat on his face and Jamie would see the pasteboard and the fake. And there was nothing anyone could do about it. Nothing.

"And away we go."

Bill walked past the old shoemaker shop, and the two of them turned the dark corner towards home. He heard the young kids again, pushing and yelling and laughing, and he knew they wouldn't go home for a long, long time.

Somewhere to Go

JOE WORKS WITH ME. He goes to classes at the University at night, but I have no idea what he's going to be because he's always changing his mind. I've been studying electronics with a correspondence school ever since I got out of high school five years ago. It's pretty complicated, but I've stuck with it.

Mrs. Bailey, who works in the office near the main gate keeping records and making out checks and things like that, says that the "proper nomenclature" of my "position" (she actually talks like that) is "Park Custodian." She get's mad at me when I say I'm a grave digger.

I'm not saying that's all there is to the job. Joe and I do a lot of work keeping up the cemetery, like cutting the grass and keeping the walks neat, but still the biggest part of our job is digging graves. So no matter what Mrs. Bailey calls it, I'm a grave digger.

That's my job. Like I said, I've been doing it for five years and Joe about three. We figured out once that we've dug enough graves to take care of a small town. And the work's steady—somebody's always dying—and it's not too complicated.

The only trouble with the job is how people feel about it. Like Mrs. Bailey, I mean. A lot of people feel funny about what I do, so that the only friends I really have are the guys I work with at the cemetery. Joe says he doesn't care about how people feel, but I sure do.

I like people, but every one I meet either gets all scared, or they laugh at me. I feel kind of sad about the ones who get scared (I'm not good-looking or anything, but I don't think I'm so ugly that I should scare people), but the ones that laugh make me mad. I mean, what's so funny about digging graves? Sure, it's a different kind of job, but heck, there's lots of people with different kinds of jobs. I know a guy that makes a business of horse manure! You know, for fertilizer. He comes to the cemetery lots of times with a load and God! The smell is awful!

And he's married!

I can't understand that. I can't even get a girl to come out with me.

Anyway, they shouldn't laugh. There's nothing funny about dying, so why should they laugh at grave-digging? And it's something that some people couldn't do very well, because it's more than just digging a hole, you know. You have to figure on things like what time of year it is, how wet or how frozen the ground is, and where the grave is going to be, and things like that.

And besides, the ones who think it's so funny probably don't remember that sooner or later everybody, no matter who they are, has to come to me. I'm the guy (along with Joe, of course) that's with him when everything's quiet and the crowd has gone home. I'm the guy that's around when he's getting used to the idea of being dead.

I remember saying something like that to Joe while we were busy digging a grave for some big-wig with one of the car companies.

"Joe," I said to him, "do you realize that this guy we're digging for is one of the richest men in town?"

"So what?" he said real nasty-like. He's having trouble with his girl, who says she can't stand his working in a cemetery.

"Well, doesn't it make you feel funny to think that he has to come to you at the end?"

"Funny!" he shouted. "It makes me feel sick! The capitalist pig! Even in death, he exploits the working class!" And then he spit.

I have trouble with Joe sometimes. Today, he decided he was a socialist or something, and he'd say some of the screwiest things. Like when he called me a "stupid blind dog." I didn't think I was a stupid or blind. And I certainly wasn't a dog. I didn't know what he wanted me to do to prove that I wasn't. But having him be a socialist was better than dealing with a Hindu yogi, or whatever he was a while back. As a socialist, he worked like mad, because feeling exploited made him feel like a martyr. But when he was a Hindu yogi, he'd just sit around all day with his legs folded and arms crossed and stare straight ahead, while I did all the work. No matter how I'd yell at him, he wouldn't hear me. Or at least he said he didn't.

I was hurt because he spit.

"What do you want to talk like that for, Joe?" I said. "The poor guy's dead and he's not hurting anybody."

He spit again.

Joe's a good guy, but you just can't talk to him when he's being a socialist. He's convinced he's right and won't listen to anything. Most of the time, though, I think he feels about things like I do. The sadness of it, I mean. Not only because it happens, but because you know it's going to happen, except that you never really know so that you can be ready for it.

I mean, you've got things to do, like a bill that you want to pay, or maybe a letter that should be written. Nothing's finished and nobody cares but you, because they don't know. So that just at the time you're finishing up, Mr. Jones, down the block, is swearing because somebody scraped the fender on his new Chevy. Or Mrs. Jones is bawling out the butcher because she thinks he cheated on the meat scales. See? They don't know.

But if they did know, it would be different and they might be sad and quiet and speak in whispers. And they'd remember and it wouldn't hurt so much that the sun was still shining and that all the rest of the world was going on just the way it always would. And maybe they wouldn't laugh at me.

I was thinking about this when a horse and wagon came out of the deep valley, just at the foot of the hill we were working. The wind was in back of him, so I knew right away that it was Charlie. He's the guy with the manure business. I yelled at him and walked down the hill to talk with him for a while. I stopped when I was twenty feet from his cart.

"How's business?" I yelled.

"Fine," he yelled back. "Just fine. And thank you for asking my friend, but let's not discuss it further. The day is too lovely for the discussion of business."

He took off his black derby hat and took a deep breath.

"Just smell that air, sir," he shouted.

I was and it was making me a little sick, but Charlie probably couldn't smell anything but the flowers.

"You are a lucky man, my friend, to be working amid this beauty all day," he yelled, "while I must ply my trade in the crowded, dirty streets of the city."

He reached into the suit coat pocket (he always wore a blue serge suit and a black derby hat) and pulled out a cigarette case.

"Have a cigarette?" he asked.

"No, thank you," I called back. I've always been kind of suspicious of those cigarettes. But Charlie was right, it was a beautiful day. The cemetery looked real nice. The trees were a bright green and kind of swaying. A lot of people think it's silly for a cemetery to look beautiful when it's just for dead people, but I don't.

"There's going to be a big funeral, today, Charlie," I told him.

"What?" he shouted. "Speak up. I can't hear you."

"I said, there's going to be a big funeral today!"

"That's fine," he shouted happily, "fine! It's good to see the cycle of life go through its turns. Life... death...life...death. It's good to be sure of dying."

"It's not good, Charlie! It's not good at all!"

"The world goes on," he said; he whistled at a sparrow chirping from a nearby tree. "People live and people die. And each death is like a grain of sand in the desert. It's not important, my friend. Place each death in its proper position in the whole picture of things and what is it? Nothing, just nothing. The only thing that's important is that you dig your graves and I haul my manure, until it's time for us to die, then someone can take our place. And there's always someone."

That wasn't right. I knew that wasn't right at all, but my voice was tired from shouting and I couldn't tell him.

Charlie stood up and stretched again.

"Ah, truly this is a glorious day," he shouted. He tipped his derby and picked up the reins. "Good-bye," he said and started up his horse. "Good-bye."

"Bye, Charlie," I called after him. "You're wrong but you're my only friend."

"That's as it should be. It's fitting. The manure merchant and the digger of graves."

I watched him leave. He waved to me from the gate. I waved back and returned to the top of the hill, and Joe and I waited for the funeral.

It was about six when the long funeral procession wound into the cemetery. I think it must have been the longest one I'd seen.

"He knew a lot of people," I said.

"It's Saturday," Joe grumbled. "And they're looking for somewhere to go."

The light was starting to go. Some of the trees kind of glowed. People in black moved around the hole in the ground. From up here, it looked like a bleeding cut. Heads bowed towards the ground. One head was up towards the sky—a white face, the minister's.

I looked for the wife. She was standing between two boys and leaning against the taller one. She didn't move at all, and she kept one hand up to her eyes. The smaller boy reached behind to scratch his butt.

I wondered how often people had stood around a grave at the foot of a hill. I wondered how often someone had to scratch while someone else died. I wondered how many were sad, how many were something else, how many were tired and didn't care anymore.

The wife threw what looked like a rose on the casket and stayed looking down at the bright red of it. The minister raised his hand and everyone bowed their head. The light brightened, like it sometimes does for just a little while before leaving for good, and it made all the white head-stones that went up and over the hill look whiter and like faces—sitting and watching in rows and aisles like it was a stadium.

I turned and looked towards the valley to the right.

"Look Joe," I said and pointed.

An older couple and a young girl were walking under the trees. The light made it seem as though you might be able to see through them if you wanted to. They were away from us and getting into the shadows so that it almost seemed like they floated towards the headstone, standing near the scotch pine that I planted last year. They stood with clasped hands for a minute and then knelt to bless the ground.

"Fools," Joe said, "they should forget the dead." And he looked away quickly, picking up a pebble to throw at a lonely sparrow. He scared it off.

"Why, Joe?" I asked. "What would they do on the weekend if they didn't come here?"

The Lost Sister

HE LOOKED DOWN at his wife, planting a new batch of bright pansies as she knelt by the grave, her hands browned from the moist earth. Earth of the grave, he thought; it seemed so strange that they should be concerned with a grave. He still longed to know what had happened, by what law of nature or God had they exchanged their cheerful, living world of air, sun, and laughter for the dank, carefully measured plot of dirt upon which so many of their tears had fallen.

He looked over at his daughter. Standing with her hands clasped before her, she stared quietly down at her mother and her older sister's grave. She looked older, quieter now. She understood better than he; she slept in her sister's room, and now would occasionally find in the closet a shoe that didn't fit her foot, or a letter she was never meant to read. She knew, quietly and solemnly, how her heart jumped when she walked into the room and no one followed. She'd heard laughter that could never be echoed, and was discovering an unending stream of the everyday details of living and growing up that were now only a constant reminder that those things had ended for someone else.

They stood on the side of a small hill rising from a macadam road that wound deeper into the cemetery. Six slender oaks rose atop the hill, dancing their sad, lonely dance with the wind against the arching blue sky and stretching long, thick shadows over the white headstones. The sun gently bathed the raw scars in the earth, working with Time to begin the healing work of grass.

The mother finished planting the pansies and stood up.

"Look, Alice," she said, pointing to a nearby grave.

It was a tiny child's grave. The earth had been recently closed. A tiny wreath of flowers had been laid against the headstone, and at the foot of the grave, a small doll with an arm torn off stared blankly towards the slender oaks and the blue sky.

It's all so strange, he thought. Mother, she'd said one day, I have a terrible pain in my side. Is it my appendix? They took her to the hospital and the doctors operated the next day. When they came to visit her, she was all excited and thrilled about her operation; she talked about how peculiar it had felt to be under the anesthetic, about the shock it had been to come awake.

Then the doctor came into the room and asked the parents to step into the hall. And there he told them that they had discovered something more than just a diseased appendix. It seemed there was a tumor, a malignant tumor. One that would spread and grow, one that would resist the sharpest knife, that would come back again and again like Evil. It would keep growing stronger as their daughter grew weaker, living and eating at her body until at the height of its power, it killed the sweet living thing even as at the cost of its own life.

Your daughter will die in six months, the doctor had said and turned away, calloused by familiarity with the science of life and death and having no desire to watch a novice learn of dying.

He remembered his wife's scream; a sob-choked, frightened denial of this last stage of existence—a denial of religious beliefs and the panicky desire to hold on to all that was known and could be felt. She began sobbing loudly, moaning in a way he'd never heard. He thought he had never known her before, he never knew she was capable of such sorrow and suffering. He became frightened.

"Stop, Mother, stop, Jessie will hear you," he'd whispered as he took her into his arms. But she didn't hear him; she was completely mesmerized by her grief.

"Jessie mustn't know, Mother, please. Jessie mustn't know." And he was surprised to feel warm tears flowing down his own cheeks, as they stood in the hallway, holding one another.

When they walked back into the room, Jessie was laughing at some joke Alice had just told her. But Alice was staring at them with grave, solemn eyes in which he could read the grief he had grown so familiar with in just one minute. All the grief the world has ever suffered through its eons waits to be suffered again in one minute of sorrow.

*****

A SMALL BOY of three sat down on a nearby headstone, kicking his heels against the stone and picking at his nose. His mother rushed to him with a horrified expression on her face and pulled him off so hard his little face began to tighten and his mouth opened in a loud wailing sob.

Let the boy sit, the man wanted to say, let him sit. It's just stone, something without feeling.

"George, it's terrible," said his wife, as her dirt-stained hand strayed absently over her cheek. "It's just terrible. I don't think they've trimmed the grass once."

"Let the grass grow."

The Ballad of Joe Hill

W HERE OTHER MEN of his generation sang "*The Road to Mandalay*" in the shower, Clarence preferred union songs. But once out of the shower, he would put on his outer skin— a dark blue vested suit, a sober tie, and a somber expression—and march solemnly, like a corporate priest, to his job with the Hansen Motor Company.

He was a company lawyer, specializing in arbitration cases. A tall bulky man, he bore an impressive, leonine head and a waistline of heroic dimensions. People who liked him said he was powerfully-built, a perfect corporate image: serious, grave, responsible, a solid rock to build on. Those who didn't—thin Ivy Leaguers for the most part—said he was fat, and a fake.

"You know, he really isn't one of us," they would whisper nasally.

It was true that after arguing the company's case—cases that he won far more often than he lost—he enjoyed nothing more than retiring with his union counterparts to some obscure bar where they could drink beer, play a little pinball and sing loud, raucous union songs. He felt at home, and totally relaxed—a vest-loosened fat man drinking beer.

"Is he one of us?" the union men would wonder. "Or is he a company spy?"

Only his wife Alice—a small, wiry woman, who wore her hair in a pony tail, read the Partisan Review, and got an A in Abnormal Psychology at State—knew her husband for what he really was: a nut.

Perhaps because of his strange Jekyll-and-Hyde existence, Clarence had developed an equally strange belief.

He was convinced that his car was out to get him.

He'd always credited inanimate objects with living a malevolent, secret life. Chairs rearranged themselves at night so that he'd trip over them in the dark; slippers were always hiding themselves; pens loved to vomit ink into his breast pocket. Then gradually, through his years with Hansen, a suspicion grew that his car disliked him. It would show up in the little things: an engine that stalled at an intersection, tires that went flat at the most awkward times. They were irritating things, but hardly vicious, at first.

It was different with the arrival of his new 1961 Hansen. As soon as he saw it, Clarence knew that this car was different: it sat there sullenly, crouched low like a poisonous toad, measuring him through its insolent headlamps. The brow of its hood was low and coarse with chrome, and the grille wore the imprint of a loutish sneer. When he looked from the side, the sneer turned into a snarl, posing like an over-dressed poolroom tough, daring him to a game of chicken.

"I swear, Alice," he once said to his wife, "that smart-aleck car waited—*waited* !—until I got on the expressway before it conked out. Now why did it wait?"

"You forgot to fill the tank and it ran out of gas," Alice replied.

"Yes, but why on the expressway? During the rush hour. Why not before? And why did it sneer at the time, like it was enjoying the mess?"

No matter what his wife tried to tell him, Clarence couldn't shake the knowledge that his car was lying in wait for him. And by winter, he had his proof.

IT WAS AFTER the first heavy snowfall and Clarence was backing the car down their narrow, one-martini driveway (he'd measured it carefully, and with two martinis he ran the risk of running into the neighbor's house). He was handling his part of the job very carefully, when one of the rear wheels, deliberately and with malice aforethought, left the cement and buried itself in the banked wet snow on the front lawn. He rocked it, pleaded with it, swore at it, but it would not give up. Thinking quickly, Alice hurried their three-year-old son into the den and turned the television as loud as she could while the boy's father filled the air with many of the the oldest, shortest words in the language. Defiantly, the car just fish-tailed further and further into the front lawn until, finally, Clarence had to admit defeat.

Even the man from the auto club was shocked. The car had wedged itself in the driveway. Sideways. Rear bumper jammed into the brick of Clarence's house, front bumper inches away from the face brick of the neighbor's house. The man from the auto club had to call in extra equipment for the job, and Clarence spent the whole rest of the day outside, doing what he could to help. Shortly thereafter, the poor auto club mechanic left town, and went to live with his maiden aunt in Encino, California. Within two years, he was raising bees and letting his beard grow.

Through the rest of the winter and on into spring, the secret battle went on, grim and unrelenting, with each side claiming minor victories through the ensuing skirmishes. Through it all, Clarence sang his union songs in the shower, buckled on his dark blue vested wool armor, and learned other labor songs at his dingy little bar. But always the question nagged him: when would the rumble come? And how?

*****

THE SHOWDOWN CAME after a party at his boss's house.

The party was only for the most favored members of the Industrial Relations Staff. To be invited was an honor since the Chief of Industrial Relations entertained so rarely. Aside from the annual "Calvin Coolidge Ball" he sponsored, he was practically a recluse.

Clarence had been nervous, about both the party and the machinations of his enemy. To steady himself, he had a couple of shots at the bar. His nerves steadied, when he got home he had a few more to relax. Relaxed, he felt warm, so he took off his vest. And he started to feel comfortable. By the time he and Alice arrived at the party, he felt completely at home and wondered where the pinball machine was.

At three in the morning, when Alice convinced Clarence that it was time to leave, he was happy and content with himself. He wasn't sure why, because the events of the evening were a bit cloudy, but he was sure he'd acquitted himself well. It didn't even bother him when the car peevishly ran over the birdbath on the front lawn.

It didn't bother him because the moon was out and the hills looked beautiful and the trees were pale and danced slowly when the breeze asked them to. And the car growled low and deep, and the flowers by the passing restaurants were all beautiful.

"Isn'itbeautiful," he rhapsodized. It came out as one word, but Alice didn't seem to notice.

"Hmph," she said.

He had scintillated, he mused. His mind had worked like a well-oiled machine, imbuing his conversation with brilliance, lending it precision, sparking it with flashes of his subtle wit.

He hummed a few lines of *"Picket Line Priscilla"* and then snapped on the radio.

Woodward was empty, temptingly so. The moon was in the sky and they were rolling towards Birmingham. He thought about challenging the car to a race to see which of them would chicken out first. But it might upset Alice, so he decided not to.

He tried to glance at her tenderly, but discovered that his eyes had started blinking individually. He tried to puzzle it out, but they were passing through Birmingham and he had to concentrate, because some of the streets cut through at odd angles. He was happily humming the *"Blue Danube Waltz"* along with the car radio, which was playing *"Tea for Two Cha-Cha,"* when Alice made an observation.

"Clare," she said simply, "you were a drunken slob."

He tried to assume an affronted air but, unfortunately, just hiccuped.

"My dear, you have obviously been drinking to excess tonight," he said, carefully choosing his words, and giving his tongue plenty of time to feel for each of them.

"A fat, drunken slob," she continued.

"Oh yeah?" he replied. His mind churned with snappy comebacks, but the only one his brain could sort out was: "That's what you think."

"Turn here," she said. And Clarence turned right sharply off Woodward Avenue onto Coolidge. The tires squealed and Clarence leaned hard on the door, which started to rattle. He felt a cold chill. The car hadn't given up yet. Obviously, he'd have to be careful. He opened the door and slammed it shut and sped through a traffic signal, barely beating the yellow light.

"Tell me, Clare," Alice resumed quietly. "Tonight of all nights, did you really have to do your imitation of a male hippopotamus courting a mate? You're certainly built for the male lead. But I don't think it was wise to pick your boss's wife for the love interest."

Clarence had forgotten that bit. He was a little shocked that he had dared. But mostly, he was awed. All the way through Berkley, he remained awed. And then the beauty of it began to shine through, and Clarence snickered.

"If I were a male hippo," he giggled, "she certainly would have fooled me."

Like a door opening, that part of the evening came alive again, and he giggled his way past Huntington Woods and on through Oak Park.

They crossed Eight Mile Road and passed into Detroit, where Coolidge Road turned into Schaefer.

"You want me to take the sitter home?" Alice asked.

"Of course not. I can do it. I want you to rest." He leered at her.

"Wipe that sexy hippo look off your face," Alice scowled. "You'll only fall asleep."

He tried leering again, but his eyes still hadn't gotten in phase, so he gave it up with a grunt. He stopped, but just barely, for a light at Seven Mile.

"And another thing, Clare," Alice said thoughtfully. "I don't think the V-P in charge of Industrial Relations for the Hansen Motor Company is all that interested in how many stanzas of 'I Dreamed I Saw Joe Hill Last Night' have been recorded. And honestly now, do you really and truly think that he wanted to hear you sing every single one? I mean, maybe he was just being polite when he sat there, listening with his mouth open like that."

"I didn't do that," he hiccupped.

"You did," she said.

THE LITTLE BOY had been no trouble at all, the baby sitter said when they woke her up. A perfect angel. And they could call her anytime. Clarence helped her into her coat and guided her towards the front door. At the door, Alice asked him another question.

"Did you know you sat on their bathroom sink?"

"You mean...?"

"Ripped the whole cotton-picking mess right out of the wall, Fatso," she said and slammed the door.

"Is it fun being a lawyer?" the babysitter wanted to know. Clarence hiccupped again and led her to the car.

TO GET THE babysitter home, Clarence drove west on Outer Drive and turned north on Schaefer to one of the side streets past Seven Mile. By the time he started back, it was after four o'clock.

The car purred with sinister efficiency. The streets were deserted. The whole city was asleep. He was out alone with a monster and where was everybody? He drove considerably above the posted speed limit and sang songs.

I dreamed I saw Joe Hill last night
Alive as you and me,
Says I, "But Joe, you're ten years dead"
"I never died," says he.

As he approached Seven Mile, the light turned red. It seemed silly to stop—everyone was asleep, after all—so he slowed down to a cautious forty-five, looked both ways very carefully, and sped on through.

His boss's wife did look like a female hippo, he chuckled.

"The copper bosses killed you, Joe.
They shot you, Joe," says I.
"Takes more than guns to kill a man,"
Says Joe, "I didn't die."

It was exhilarating, being alone and above the law. And singing union songs. His boss should sing them, Clarence thought; he'd understand his job better.

And standing there as big as life.
And smiling with his eyes,
Joe says, "What they forgot to kill
Went on to organize."

The intersection at Six Mile and Schaefer was the center of an big shopping center. On the southeast corner was a department store, on the southwest, a group of small stores: a men's shop, a record emporium, and a hardware store. The two other corners were occupied by a drug store and a gas station.

The light was green as Clarence approached the intersection. But it had been green for a while, so he stomped down on the gas pedal. The car leapt forward eagerly, the engine roaring a brisk "Tally-ho!"

Nearing the corner, he noticed a big black car parked by the department store corner, with a red light on top that went round and round and round and the word "Police" written in big white letters on the side. He looked to see that the caution light was yellow now, and he seemed to recall it being that way for quite some time.

In the instant before reaching the corner, a surge of adrenalin brought a flash of sobriety to his brain. Suddenly, Clarence found himself stone-cold sober, with all his well-oiled mental faculties feverishly at work, considering what to do. His brain raced along in high gear; slowed down to the level of mortals, his superhuman thought process ran something like this:

> I'm going way too fast. They know it and I know it. And on top of that, I've been drinking. I could get into real trouble.
>
> If I keep going straight, I'll just *'whoosh'* past them and it'll make everything sound even faster. And I can't possibly slow it down enough so that it won't go *'whoosh.'* So—?
>
> So I'll just make a quick right turn onto Six Mile and everything will be just fine.

He made the turn. The tires squealed and he was thrown heavily against the door.

The next thing he knew, he was bouncing down Six Mile on his rump, his legs still flexed in a driving position and both hands curled tightly around a phantom steering wheel.

When he stopped bouncing, he continued to sit, squinting at the men's shop through suddenly blurry eyes. At least, he thought it was a men's shop. Then a blizzard of white shirts started falling over everything, and he worried about going snow blind as the shirts rose and fell, wafting gently over the hood of a car whose door on the driver's side was wide open. But it didn't really look like a car, he noticed; it looked more like a pile of junk. A dead pile of junk.

Two policemen were suddenly squatting in front of him, asking if he was all right.

He removed one hand from the phantom steering wheel to scratch his head. "I'm fine," he said. "But I seem to have misplaced my car."

Puzzled, he looked around.

"Don't bother looking for it, though. I'll just walk."

Mr. Leitmitov

THE FUNERAL PARTY at the cemetery had been a small one. Some of Eli's friends hadn't come because they didn't want to be reminded of death; others hadn't come because they were already with the dead.

But Mr. Leitmitov and the Chesniks had come, as always, just as in the past they had come to the weddings and the christenings.

Alex Chesnik was a heavy, dark man with a naked forehead and glowering eyes; his hands were strong-looking and curved as though remembering a tool. Anna, his wife, had stood beside him. She was a small, round woman with a pretty face; her eyes were filled with tears and she held a handkerchief pressed against her mouth.

Leitmitov had stood across from them, near the birch tree at the head of the grave. He was a thin pale man with meek, blue eyes under quizzically arched eyebrows; his shirt collar was laundry-stiff and white against the neat blackness of a severely buttoned topcoat. He held a smoothly blocked hat in his thin, white hands. His light, thinning hair was carefully parted and combed to hide a bald spot. He was the only one of the small party who stood without a woman beside him.

It had been a blustery day. Shredded gray clouds traveled fast across the sky, and shriveled brown leaves scuttled across the ground like crabs, darting into the raw hole in the ground. Mr. Leitmitov's eyes had met Alex's across Eli's open grave. Like a reflex, his quick, ingratiating smile had flicked on. But it faded quickly when he realized that neither he nor Alex was seeking the other, but were instead seeing all the friends that had gone. And his smile had flickered, like a neon sign gone bad.

THE SMALL LAWN in front of the Chesnik house was covered with leaves from the trees and shrubs, which stirred under the light breeze. After he had locked the car, Alex joined Anna and Leitmitov on the sidewalk. Spreading his arms wide, he invited both of them to inspect the lawn. "See!" he said in Russian. "See! A grown son in the house and still it looks like this!" Where was he, Alex wanted to know. Walter would be back later with his girl, his wife told him, but Alex kept grumbling and didn't hear.

In the house, Anna Chesnik took the coats from the men, hung them up and went into the kitchen to fix some food. Alex rumbled to clear his throat and told Leitmitov to sit in the living room. He went into the dining room and took a whiskey bottle and two shot glasses from the heavy, dark buffet, joined his friend on the red mohair sofa and set up two shots on the dark mahogany coffee table in front of him.

The two old friends sat in silence. Occasionally, Alex parted the lace curtains to peer out at the street. It had grown more windy and bleakly dark; the skeleton trees sang of the dark wind, and an old Russian song kept running through Leitmitov's mind.

How many times have I sat here, sat here?
How many times must I grieve?
How many leaves has the wind blown, wind blown?
How many friends will I leave?

They had two more shots. The drinks flushed Leitmotiv's face, but the warm glow never came.

The warm smell of stuffed cabbage filled the house, and Anna was setting the massively dark dining room table for dinner. She had used her table cloth of Polish linen and the setting for two she had collected at some movie theater a long time ago. She ate in the kitchen.

Besides the cabbage, there was cold Polish sausage with horseradish that Anna had grated herself, and potatoes mashed with onions. Alex set the whiskey on the table and they had a couple of more shots during the meal.

But Leitmitov didn't feel like eating. Even the stuffed cabbage, which he always liked, he ate only because he didn't want Anna to think that he didn't like her cooking. He just couldn't get over how quickly it had happened. Eli had always been sickly—since he was a boy!—so how could anyone know that this last sickness was so bad?

"How old was he, anyway?" Leitmitov asked, after he swallowed the last piece of sausage on his plate. He spoke the cultivated Russian that had always impressed the ladies of the colony, and irritated the men because it seemed so affected.

"Eli?" Alex crossed his knife and fork on the plate, pushed the plate away and leaned his head back to frown thoughtfully at the ceiling. "I think he was fifty-six." He looked to the door leading into the kitchen. "Anna!" he called. His Russian was spoken with the coarser accent of the peasant. The coarseness was a habit he'd fallen into when conversing with Leitmitov. Long ago, it had started as a rebuff to his friend to remind him that both of them had come from the same peasant village.

Anna came to the door, wiping her hands in a dish towel and chewing her last bite of food.

"Eli was fifty-six, no?" Mr. Chesnik asked.

She cocked her head thoughtfully, brought a finger up to her pursed lips very slowly, and considered.

"Well? Well? Yes or no?" her husband asked impatiently.

"No," she decided, "I think in December he would have been fifty-six. Yes, I'm sure of it, because I remember his birthday was always exactly one month after Walter's." Alex grunted, and she returned to her dinner in the kitchen.

"He would have been fifty-six in December," Alex said to his friend. He poured them two more shots. Leitmitov threw his down, and felt the heat but nothing more. He passed his hand over his head, fingering some loose strands into place of the bald spot.

"That's only two years older than me," Leitmitov said. He shook his head. It didn't seem right, he thought. Dying friends should be ten or fifteen years older. His faulty smile flicked on and was gone. "How many are left from the old village now, Alex?"

Alex looked surprised. His friend was using the country accent of the peasant.

"Just you and me and Paul on the farm up north."

"So, if there was six of us who come to this country together, that means Eli and Peter and John are gone."

Alex stirred uncomfortably in his chair and nodded his head.

There had been six of them, Leitmitov was thinking. Six laughing young men, bound for America. Their songs had been of love and courage and fulfillment. And on the boat coming over, he had been the strong one, the eager one. He'd sung them sad songs, because he was happy, and he had made them cry. Six young men. Their songs became dark, lonely songs, songs of regret and forever. One was a suicide at thirty, another was killed in a bar fight at forty, and now it was Eli, the gentle one.

Now, he couldn't even remember what Eli looked like. All he could remember was the mound of earth that looked like a swelling eye over a mended hurt, and how Anna Chesnik had wiped her eyes dry, and how Alex had settled his hat on his head and then beckoned him to follow.

He had been surprised that it was done, and as he followed the Chesniks, he looked back, almost expecting someone to point out that they were leaving someone behind. But there had been nothing. Just this mound of earth over which the leaves stumbled.

"HE LAY IN that room three days before they came to him," Leitmitov mused. "They said he smelled. That's why they kept the coffin closed. The smell and the change."

Alex grimaced. "Why are you talking about it?" he asked uncomfortably.

"I know it's not nice to talk about," Leitmitov said softly, "but I was thinking about something. Don't you think it was funny that they didn't find any money?"

His friend snorted. "That's not so funny," he said. "I don't have any money either."

Leitmotiv shook his head in disagreement.

"No, Alex, it is funny," he insisted. "I think someone stole the money while he was lying there."

"That's crazy now! That's just crazy talk!"

"But it would be so easy."

"In the first place, who would want to do such a thing, eh? And in the second place, Eli never had much money anyway. So let's not talk about it anymore, all right?"

"But listen, Alex— "

"Listen nothing! He is dead and he is buried. It makes no difference now. Don't talk of what has happened. There isn't time enough for that." Scowling, he got up and walked around the table.

"Come on," he said, tugging gently at his friend's arm. "Come on. Let's sit in the front room. I can get Walter's guitar and we'll sing some songs."

Alex went into the son's room and came out with the guitar. He was wiping the dust off with his hand.

"Over one hundred dollars for his guitar and lessons," he grumbled, "and he never touches it anymore." He strummed it and flinched at the discordant sound. He walked to the sofa in the living room and beckoned to his friend to join him. "And bring the bottle," he said.

Leitmitov delivered the bottle of whiskey and sat down beside Alex on the sofa. Gently, he placed a hand on his friend's shoulder.

"Alex," he asked, "will you let Anna hold my money for me?"

Alex slammed at the strings of the guitar and swore.

"What can you do with such a man!?" he demanded loudly. "Like a phonograph record, over and over, he sings the same song. No! No, I will not let Anna hold your money! No!"

Anna Chesnik had come into the dining room to clear the table. The dishes had been stacked on the buffet and she was carefully gathering up the table cloth when her husband's outburst interrupted her. She wanted to know what the trouble was.

"He wants you to hold his money," Alex told her.

"I don't want someone stealing it," Leitmitov explained. "I live alone, like Eli. I have no one to wake me up for work, or to feel my head for a fever. And I don't want my friends to pay for my funeral."

Anna's face had lost its big-cheeked roundness; it had a crumbled, shrunken look. She tightened her lips and shook her head very hard.

"Don't talk that way!" she finally said, in a trembling, throaty voice. "Stop it! Nobody's dying!" Her eyes shone big and round, and she swallowed painfully. She bit down on her lower lip to check its trembling.

Leitmitov was flustered by her reaction. He stood up, his face red, and bowed very stiffly towards Anna, turning on his smile for her and then for his friend, Alex. He sat down again, smiling at nothing.

"Here," Alex said gruffly, handing him the guitar, "tune up the guitar. All the strings are run down." He watched Leitmitov begin and then added, "You are in too much of a hurry. We just had a funeral today. That should be enough for a while."

"You shouldn't joke about it," Anna protested from the dining room where she was finishing up. "It's not good to joke about things like that." Her husband waved his hand in a gesture of dismissal and turned to Leitmitov and the guitar.

*****

THEY SANG A few songs together, Mr. Leitmotiv's soft tenor riding lightly on Alex Chesnik's rumbling bass. Then Leitmitov suddenly thought of a song he hadn't thought of in years, and sang it alone.

> *When I can see the birch tree, birch tree,*
> *Will she be waiting there?*
> *Or will it be a sad tree, sad tree,*
> *With branches starkly bare?*

And as he sang, he was suddenly the young soldier in the song, and he was young and strong and straight and his hair was curly and thick and everyone was there just the way they had always been. He was in his mother's house and Mama stood by the table with the big pot of soup and she looked at him when he came through the doorway and his father and brother shouted his name and Mama started crying and covering her face with one hand and reaching blindly for him with the other and from the back a pretty girl called his name and begged him to look at her and he saw the lovely white dress shining in the moonlight and—

"Why did you stop?" the Chesniks both asked. Anna's cheeks were wet.

"It was so beautiful," she said.

Alex blew his nose loudly and wiped his eyes. "It was very nice," he said. "How did you remember that old song?"

"I don't know," Leitmitov answered. "I don't know." His hand trembled as he passed it over his hair, his fingers worrying the bald spot again. He felt hot, and the room was starting to swim in and out of focus.

He didn't want to sing anymore, he told them, because he was feeling the whiskey a little bit. Alex put the guitar away and Anna picked up her sewing basket to do some mending. Leitmitov studied her fingers managing the thread, the fingers moving so that a glint of gold flicked off the thick wedding band. He kept the fingers in focus. There was a loud and steady thump in his chest, and he realized it was his heart. It would be nice, he thought, to have a good woman. And the song came back and the girl kept calling his name. And he tried to hear, but the wind was moaning in the trees and weeping down the rain spouts. And his heart thumped and thumped.

*****

A CAR PULLED up in front of the house. Leitmitov was carefully turning to look at his friend, when Anna came between them, kneeling on the sofa to peek through the curtains.

"Here they come," she said breathlessly.

"They? Who? Walter and someone?" Alex asked.

"Well sure! His girl!" she replied impatiently. She snatched up the bottle and glasses and hid them behind the sofa. Her husband was looking at her blankly.

"I told you before," she said. "Pay attention next time."

"No, you didn't tell me before," he insisted, brushing at his hair. Leitmitov's face was masked by his automatic smile, but no one was looking at him.

There were footsteps coming up the front steps, a murmur of voices and then, a girl's soft shy laugh. It was like a signal. The room came into sharp focus and everything stopped, and Leitmitov saw everything as if it were a picture.

Alex and Anna Chesnik were standing, staring towards the front door. Alex had his hands in his pockets and a scowl on his face, but his lips were parted and half-smiling; Anna placed one hand on her heart and the other hand up to her smiling mouth; her eyes were shining.

The front door opened and Walter entered the house with a girl. She was a small, dark-haired girl with very serious eyes and an uncertain, smiling mouth. And the thump came back and the room began to dance. Leitmitov sat, watching and listening in silence as voices rose around him.

This was Martha, this was mother, they were saying. There were tears all around, and everyone reaching and embracing and kissing, with the warmth and pride of four people coming sharply into focus.

Leitmitov felt as if he were far away, looking at them through a telescope. And so he stood up.

"I must go," he said.

"My gosh," Walter exclaimed. "We haven't introduced you. Martha, this is Mr. Leitmitov. And old friend of the family." He grinned at his father. "You should hear him play the guitar."

The girl smiled at him.

She said, how nice it was to meet him, and that she would like to hear him play the guitar sometime because Walter said he played so well.

"I have to go," said Leitmitov. "I have something to do early tomorrow, so I have to go. Some other time, maybe."

Alex came to him and walked him into the vestibule. He helped him on with his coat, asking if he was all right.

"I'm fine."

"For sure?"

"For sure."

The girl was laughing at something that Walter had said, and Anna hugged her again.

"If you still want it," said Alex, "I will let Anna keep your money for you."

Beyond them, the girl's voice was a soft, soothing murmur.

"We will talk about it some other time," his friend answered. "You shouldn't have my funeral money in your house now."

"Well, goodnight then."

"Goodnight, Alex," Leitmitov said, and then he called out to the three people still standing in the living room. The girl had her back to him. "Good night everyone." The girl half turned, the point of her chin almost touching her white blouse at the shoulders, and she smiled a soft goodbye as he stood in the shadows of the vestibule.

OUTSIDE, on the porch, Leitmitov listened to the wind, watching the brittle naked trees move stiffly against the moonlit sky, and he was remembering.

She had been dressed in white and was going up the stairs of the house and the trees had creaked with the wind. She had stopped to look back at him, as he hid himself in the shadows, her chin turning to look over her shoulder, her eyes shining with moonlight and tears. Look at me, she had said softly. I will miss you, she said. And then he rushed away down the dusty street. He heard his name called, and the wind had torn and scattered the sound, and he pretended it had never come. But looking back towards the corner, he had seen the white of her dress and the shadows dancing and swaying over it. Stay, she had said; stay. I want you to stay, she had said.

Reaching the sidewalk, Leitmitov looked back at the Chesnik house. It is such a little thing, he thought, to have someone wake you for work, or feel your head for the fever.

He shivered at the sound the leaves made scuttling across the sidewalk and started towards the bus stop.

The Lavender Unicorn

FOR BILLY WILSON, AGE EIGHT, it was waking up slowly that always began the soft, foggy adventure of rising to a Saturday morning. Leisurely, pleasantly, he considered the matter of the bed. It was his, he smiled. From there, everything fell into line. The room was his and it was morning; the light was prodding at his closed eyes, and his ears were tickled by the early murmurings of a day preparing itself for play.

He stayed under the covers, relishing a few extra minutes in the warm privacy of his bed. This was Saturday. But it was a special Saturday, unlike any other that had ever come before. From the warm dark valley of his bed, he wondered about the specialness of Saturdays, trying his best to explain the flurry of excitement that was racing in his brain and pumping in his stomach. Was the last Saturday special too? he wondered. Yes it was, but in a different way. Completely different, making the two days, though each bore the same name, total strangers. The light in the room was different; the sounds floating in from the outside were different. Even his pajamas felt different. And even he, he knew in his heart, was different.

But there was the dream....

He sat up with a start, and looked quickly towards the windows, expecting anything and being amazed by the sameness of the outside. His bedroom curtains stirred lazily under a gentle breeze. The square of his window was filled by the hazy, fluttering green of the trees, and the light from the sun was gold and heavy with the promise of a satisfying, exciting adventure.

He wondered if it really was a dream. But it was a dream that had seemed real—the scent of night greeting him at the window, the willow tree pale under the saddened moonlight, and a man who looked like his father running barefoot over the grass, leaping and laughing at the moon.

There had been a party, he remembered, with important people. Someone his father worked for, Billy thought; and his mother wouldn't let him come downstairs because he might say some silly things. That man was there, too—the oily one who laughed too much. The one who sometimes came to the house during the day, on days when Billy always had to stay outside. At least until the oily man left.

He recalled that Mother had been tucking him in when Father walked into the room and stood looking down until she finished, holding a glass in his hand. In the dark of the room it looked as though Father was swaying from side to side. Mother stood up and whispered something to him about being careful, about not having too much. He smiled at her and drank from the glass, and then smiled at her again.

"Take it downstairs," Father had said, handing her the glass, "and let our guests see their beautiful hostess." And she was beautiful, Billy thought, in her long white dress. Warm and beautiful. But she turned away quickly and left the room. She didn't say goodnight, and didn't even kiss him. Father sat on the edge of the bed.

"She didn't kiss me," Billy had said.

"Your mother's real busy, son," Father had answered. "Maybe she'll be back later. Maybe." He patted Billy's shoulder. Only he missed it once or twice and his hand landed on Billy's face. It was funny, and Billy laughed.

"You hit my nose!" he exclaimed, still laughing.

"I did?" his father had asked, looking surprised. "Well now, how did that happen I wonder? Must be your big nose keeps getting in the way."

He laughed and bent down, rubbing a rough cheek against Billy's. Laughing, Billy protested and his father rose to get up, placing one hand on the bed as though afraid of falling. He laughed deeply, his stiff white shirt shaking in the moonlight. "Go to sleep, Scout," he said, and walked towards the door. It was a funny walk, Billy remembered. Like he was going through deep water, or through a dark room and afraid of bumping his nose. At the door, Father stayed with his hand on the light switch and slowly blinked both eyes at Billy. Then he snapped the switch and the lamp beside the bed went out. The door opened, and light from the hall spilled into the room; then, the door closed and Billy was alone with the darkness.

Billy dug deeper into the warm darkness of his bed, retreating from morning while deciding whether what happened had been a dream or not.

Where did the dream start, he wondered. It was after the darkness became thick and heavy, and he lost himself in it. The bureau and the desk and the clock and the chairs had all turned into something else, and strange beings drifted through the room, whispering to him, inviting him to enter dark mysteries of a wild, ancient world. Darkness came over everything and everything dissolved into something else, and he wondered where was he going, and whether daylight would ever come again. If he shut his eyes, he discovered, it would be dark inside; he and the darkness would be the same, and then nothing could happen.

But then he heard laughter outside. Women and men were all laughing at something. And weaving through the chorus, he heard the sound of his mother's unhappy laugh—a laugh filled with anger and shame.

And then in his dream (although if he thought real hard, he seemed to remember struggling out of bed and towards the window), he suddenly found himself looking down into his backyard. He could see the rich moonlight on the wet grass, and drops of moisture sparkling on the lace of the young willow tree. And his father, his hair all rumpled and wearing a soiled white shirt and pants rolled up to his knees, was standing barefoot in the middle of the lawn, pointing off into the dark shadows beyond the yard.

"Look!" Father cried, his heavy-lidded eyes wide and happy. "Look at the unicorn! By God! A real unicorn!"

But the laughter kept building, wave upon wave of cruel, dark laughter. And the barefoot man stood, his lonely arms hanging limply at his sides, his head bent a little, staring at the people all laughing. Then he threw back his head and laughed at the sky; and then he bent over, clutching his middle, and laughing at the earth.

In his dream, Billy slowly crept away from the window, the palm of one hand wet with the moisture on the sill, tears wetting his cheeks. He didn't know why the tears had come, because he was happy for his father, and happy for the unicorn.

Sitting on his bed, Spring and the new day were pouring through the open window. He stared at his hand. It was dry. His cheeks were dry. It must have been a dream.

But what was a unicorn?

Suddenly a robin was on the window sill, nervously inspecting the interior and alert for any tricks. It hopped along the edge, apparently considering coming into the room. Wavering on the edge, its better judgment seemed to be pulling it away, and after a minute or two the bird flew away into the sun-drenched outside.

Billy smiled at the wonder of it. The painful, sad, yet wondrous magic of it—and the day had just started! He wondered fearfully, delightedly, where the coming hours would take him.

He got out of his bed, thinking of the robin, and the magic that was Saturday, and the dream that was the unicorn. But especially the robin now, because it was the robin's visit that had made the day all his own. It was now a day created by the special person called Billy Wilson, and all its magic ingredients for a special Saturday were his to shape and mold however he chose. He wondered if he could tell anyone, and let them share the wonder and excitement. Mother and Father, maybe...should he tell them?

Slowly shaking his head, he stripped his pajamas and reached for his shorts. Grownups could be very strange, he thought. They never seemed to understand the importance of important things. They were always missing what they shouldn't miss and seeing what they shouldn't see. They would take this for a regular Saturday; they wouldn't see that he had made it, and that it was a miraculous creation—like the white, warm egg that he sometimes found in the chicken house and held gently in his cupped hands.

Putting on his blue jeans, he paused and looked towards the window. Maybe he could tell his father, he thought. But never his mother.

"Billy! Come right down here. We're waiting breakfast."

"I'm coming, Mom!"

He tied his shoe laces into very neat, precise knots—just as he'd been taught—and stood up to look down at them before slipping his T-shirt over his head.

As he walked towards the door, Billy was surprised by a sudden, profound silence outside. The breeze had disappeared and gone to other, distant trees, and the leaves lay quiet, motionless. Birds, noisily exchanging views on the coming day just a moment before, were now hushed and secretive. Billy stepped to the window and stuck his head out. He stared down at the willow tree. It was the youngest tree in the yard, and it was the tree in his dream. Its long delicate branches reached down to gently stroke the grass growing about it. The sunlight seemed to bathe it in a misty green. But the tree could tell him nothing of what had happened; it just accepted the silence. Billy waited, and before he could puzzle it out the birds started singing again, and the day was just as it had been.

But the silence was important, he thought.

"Billy!"

"Coming—but I've got to wash my hands."

"Hurry then! Everything's getting cold."

In the bathroom, he washed as little of his face as he could, then rubbed his face briskly with a rough towel. He avoided looking into the mirror until he had studiously hung up the towel, and then he stared into the mirror. That was his face staring back at him, he thought in wonder: red face, big eyes, big ears, funny-looking nose. But it was his own face—and it belonged to that one person who was Billy Wilson. And, he thought gravely, that person was becoming somebody else, minute by minute, hour by hour, Saturday by Saturday.

He felt himself go dizzy. This was Saturday!

Quietly, he let himself out of the bathroom and sat down on the top step of the landing. From there, he could hear Father and Mother talking. Listening was his favorite game; it was like being someplace you weren't, and hearing every-thing. One day he'd like to look into his own window, he thought, and see himself asleep, not knowing he was being watched. It was kind of like being God, he smiled.

"Really now, Bill," Mother exclaimed, "this is too much. I don't believe you're even trying to control yourself."

Billy pictured his mother: slim and young and beautiful. Even in the morning when everyone else was wrinkled and crusted with sleep.

"Must you, even before breakfast?" she exclaimed. "I should think last night would have given you your fill." Her breath made a loud, angry sound, and then she was silent, as if waiting for Billy's father to say something.

"How can you say such a thing, Madge?" Father replied at last, his voice sounding like he'd just finished swallowing something. "How could I ever get my fill?"

"But Bill...the way you acted last night. And after you promised to behave! What are those people going to think of you? Your boss and the people from Philadelphia?"

"I don't give a damn what they think," he said merrily.

"Well, you're the one that invited them. You're the one that wanted to impress them."

"Don't remind me! Scraping and smiling until my face hurt. Slapping them on the back. Calling them Art or Bert or Eddie. Trying to be like them. And I don't like any of 'em." He groaned suddenly as though stabbed by a vivid and painful memory.

"And laughing at their stupid jokes," he muttered.

"You shouldn't feel that way, Bill."

For a moment, there was nothing but silence, broken by Mother's harsh sigh. "Bill, please stop! Not another!"

"Relax, Madge," Father returned gently. "Take it easy. This is Saturday, remember? The youngest day. I don't have to think about anything for two whole days. So just relax and forget about me. Let me dream."

He laughed softly. Billy smiled to himself because his father knew about Saturday. He knew it was a special day, and wouldn't have to be told about it. It was a secret that both of them knew. The day would be theirs together, and they wouldn't need words to tangle things up.

"Barefoot!" his mother suddenly blurted. "Running barefoot on the lawn and shouting at the moon. In front of everyone!"

Billy started: *the dream!* Only it wasn't a dream anymore. It was all real—the wet on his hands, the tears. And the unicorn! The word like the sound of a deep, mellow hunting horn. The unicorn!

"They enjoyed it," his father was saying. "They laughed till they got red in the face."

"But awful laughter, Bill. Awful, dirty laughter."

"I noticed you were laughing too, Madge."

"But really. What could I....?"

"And that oily one, the oily one with his oily laugh."

"Oily...?"

"You know...your occasional house guest," he said gently. "The dark, oily house guest. The soulful-eyed oily one."

"What do you mean?" she asked in a low voice; he laughed again, a low, mirthless chuckle.

"I just think I'll have another little one," he said, the echoes of laughter dying in his voice.

"What do you mean?" she persisted. "What are you saying about me?"

"Oh nothing, Madge, for God's sakes! Don't get all dramatic about it. I really don't give a damn anymore."

A sullen silence fell, thick and unyielding. Billy wanted them to talk some more; he wanted to hear and learn something he could use when he went out to play.

"Where is that boy?" his mother asked suddenly, and pushed her chair back from the table. Billy had gotten up and was just starting down when something his father said made him stop and tremble.

"I saw a unicorn last night," Father said distantly, as if talking to himself; Mother said nothing.

"A lavender one. The color of your apron."

"I know," she answered in a taut voice. "You told us last night."

Billy came running down the stairs and dashed into the kitchen.

"Hi-ya, Billy boy!" Father grinned, and then grimaced fiercely and feinted a blow at Billy's head. Laughing with glee, the boy jumped back.

"Where have you been?" Mother asked sternly.

"Yeah," Father added with mock anger. "We were afraid you fell into the toilet and then I'd have to go down to the river to fish you out."

His father laughed, then winked both eyes heavily. Billy wanted to laugh, but his mother wasn't laughing and her face was all stern, so he decided not to. Solemnly, he sat down and drank his orange juice. And he thought about the dream and the unicorn. About waking up slowly, and the robin, and his barefooted father in the middle of the moon-soaked lawn. And about the unicorn.

"What's a unicorn?" he asked. He hadn't meant to ask the question out loud. He was thinking the question, hearing the sound of the words in his mind, when the words just came alive in his throat.

His father roared with laughter, but Mother looked at him hard.

"Billy," she asked stiffly, "you've been eavesdropping again, haven't you?"

It was terrible, he thought. They would never know any of his secret games unless his words told them. And his words were always tattling on him.

"Haven't you, Billy?" his mother repeated.

"I didn't mean to. It just happened."

She started to say something when his father interrupted. "It just happened," he laughed, and his laughter shook his whole body. "What could he do if it just happened?"

"Please Bill. Don't encourage him. It's terrible the way he's picked up the habit of snooping. You never know when he's listening around some corner, hearing I-don't-know-what."

"Just send him to the backyard when your company arrives, Madge. He can't snoop from out in the yard."

She turned quickly in her chair and faced the windows. Father smiled gently at her back and then smiled at Billy and winked both his eyes.

"You ol' rascal," he whispered, then laughed slowly. Billy choked on a laugh that almost escaped.

"So you heard?" his father asked.

Billy nodded. "Why were you barefoot?"

His father laughed again

"Because the grass was wet and I wanted to feel it between my toes. When you grow up, you always wear shoes, you know. So the grass never touches your bare feet."

And he looked at his son and smiled in a way that only Billy could understand. They held a secret between them, one that they could never say out loud. Not with anyone else in the room with them.

"And you saw a unicorn?" Billy asked. "And it was the color of that?" He pointed to his mother's apron; Father nodded, still smiling.

"What's a unicorn?"

"Don't you know?"

He shook his head.

"Well, it's an animal that most people say isn't real. They say it's make-believe. Most people say that."

"But you saw it, didn't you?"

"You bet I did! There are lots of things that people say aren't real. Beautiful things they don't see. Some ugly things are real and they think they're beautiful because they don't see anything else. The unicorn is something they say isn't but had always been."

"Don't you think it's time you stopped, Bill?" Mother asked, without turning in the chair; her voice sounded husky and full.

"No, I don't," Billy's father replied. "It's important that my son understand about these things. You do, don't you Billy?"

He didn't, but he believed that he did, because he liked to have his father talk to him this way. It was only at certain times that his father talked to him about important things like this—and he could tell they were very important from the way his father stared at him and the way his mother stared down at her plate. Other days, Father was more like the other grownups, but on these particular days—days that were coming more and more often, Billy realized happily—they could talk so that he could be included in all these important thoughts and feelings, and words that built the secrets he shared with his father. Then he became part of that secret, because he—Billy Wilson—was the only other one who could understand. The only one! Not even Mother could understand.

"What's a unicorn?" he asked.

His father grinned. "It's a creature that looks like a pony, with a twisty horn growing from right between his eyes."

Billy looked at his father for a long time. Even though it was one of those certain days, even though it was a special Saturday, the boy wondered if he was just being fooled and teased. An animal the color of his mother's apron with a twisty horn seemed much too marvelous a miracle even for a special Saturday. And grownups seemed to enjoy telling him things that weren't true, things that were just plain silly. Things like the world was round, or the sky wasn't really blue; insisting that birds couldn't really talk, or that on nights when the stars weren't there, saying that they were only hiding. But his father had never told him things that weren't true. At least, not on their special days. And yet he wondered. Maybe something had changed. So he just stared until his father smiled and winked both his eyes, and then Billy returned to his breakfast, content and happy.

It was very quiet at the table for the rest of breakfast, but Billy welcomed the silence. He was thinking long and serious thoughts—about the unicorn and the robin, the willow and the grownup world that he had spied on.

"What do you say to a walk in the woods, Scout?" his father asked.

Billy nodded quickly, hoping to make their adventure an established fact, one that was beyond calling back.

"Right," his father grunted, nodding his head in emphatic agreement.

"You were going to put up the screens, Bill," Mother said, her voice cold and distant.

"Later on, Madge! Later on! I've got all day. It's Saturday, remember? The youngest day. All we've got to think of is how much sun we can get and how much air we can breathe—eh, Billy?"

Billy nodded solemnly and his father reached across to grip him hard at the shoulder. He shook the boy gently and spoke through tightly clenched teeth: "Atta boy, Billy. You're my special little buddy."

His mother opened her mouth to speak, but stopped before saying a word. She shrugged her shoulders and stood up to stack the breakfast dishes. "Well...try to get back early," she sighed. "They should be up today."

Billy thought his mother looked sad. It was wrong for her to look sad. The day was happy and shining, but sadness was dark. It could blight a whole day and everything would grow black, crawling with things that craved the darkness.

"Don't worry about them," Father said. "Forget them until we get back. Billy and I will put them up—right, William?"

Billy nodded, breathless with pride because he had been called by his whole name, and his father smiled at his son's proud, reddened face. Then he leaned across the table and whispered loudly:

"Maybe we'll see a unicorn!"

He was smiling when he said it. But Billy noticed that, quite suddenly, the smile had vanished, and his father seemed to be staring blankly at Billy. Staring at him, but not really seeing him.

"Won't you please stop, Bill?" his mother pleaded. She was standing at the kitchen sink, her back to them, head bowed a little.

"He'll believe you," she said.

"Let him," Father answered, snapping out of his trance. "It'll be good. Everyone should have something to believe. Let it be a myth. There really isn't much else to believe in, these days."

Father turned and stared at her back. His eyes shone and a phantom smile danced over his lips. He looked like Billy sometimes felt when he was about to do something he'd been told not to do.

"I grant you that myths are fragile things," he said. His voice was serious and solemn, but Billy could hear a tiny, hidden laugh in the words. Mother heard it, too, because she quickly stiffened her back.

"The process of growing up," he continued, "is the process of breaking or losing your myths." He paused and faced Billy. He winked both his eyes and laughed. Mother turned around and Billy was puzzled by the dark look in her eyes, and the tight lines around her mouth. She suddenly looked old.

"For instance," his father said, turning and smiling at his mother. "Can you think of anything that sounds as archaic as the word—chastity?"

He laughed, amused by the word. "My God!" he exclaimed. "How strange it sounds!"

Billy felt uneasy. Something was happening, something was making everything feel tight and dangerous. Billy looked to his father, who was staring at Mother's ashen face. Her eyes were wide and staring, and her mouth hung open as if she'd been hit in the stomach. And Billy noticed a terrible sound in the room—a trembling, heavy, choked sound, that he knew was his mother's breathing. Suddenly frightened, he wanted more than anything go leave. Sternly, his father looked down at him.

"Why don't you wait outside for me, ol' boy?" his father said. And so Billy ran out the door, hungering for the outside, and eager to get away from his mother's breathing.

The glorious morning was waiting for him when he stepped outside, but he wasn't quite ready for it. He felt unclean and old, and everything was shaking beneath him. He even wondered if he really was Billy Wilson, and worried about how he could be certain that he'd really gotten out of bed that bright, promising morning. Maybe it was really dark, and he was dreaming the daylight. He sat down on the steps, wondering how he could tell, and what he could do to stop.

Some nearby sparrows started a noisy quarrel and Billy jumped in alarm. He watched them fearfully, half-expecting them to turn into something else. But they kept on being sparrows, and so the boy breathed easier, thinking that maybe nothing had really changed. Maybe things would just be different for a little while. Carefully, he checked around, looking for the rest of his day.

And he saw that things were just as he wanted them. He saw the wide lawn in back of their house, sparkling with the morning dew; he saw the young willow tree reaching towards the earth with its weak, fragile arms. And off to the right, he could see the woods; and he saw the trees beckoning him to come. They looked sweet and inviting, despite the dark mystery of their dark, blue shadows. Even the busy little cars, hurrying along the distant highway towards town, seemed right and proper, hinting at shadows and promises of other woods, other young willows that he had never seen. It seemed that everything different was inside. And because he was outside now, none of it could touch him.

Besides, it was only about his father's wanting to be happy and not putting the screens up right away. Father would fix it up so that everything would be just like it was before his mother's terrible breathing. And then a sudden thought struck him, and he stared vacantly into space as he considered it further.

Maybe, he thought, maybe she didn't like the unicorn.

With a bang of the screen door behind him, Father came out of the house. He patted a bulge in his pocket and wiped his mouth with the sleeve of his jacket. He was smiling, and the corners of his mouth quivered with his smile.

"Ah, Billy!" he exclaimed, throwing his arms wide and turning his face up to the sun. "What a day for Saturday! Everything turning soft and kind."

He looked down at Billy. "You know what I used to do when I was a little boy and a day like this came?"

Billy shook his head and his father shook his head back at him.

"You're going to think I was silly," his father whispered, "but I'm going to tell you anyway. I used to take off my shoes and go looking for the softest, muddiest ground I could find. Then I'd step into it and let the warm stuff ooze through my toes and over my feet. Then I'd spread my arms and pretend I was a tree. It was funny. I could almost feel my feet—they were roots, you understand—sucking up food from the ground. And I used to think the birds would come, and we'd be friends."

He fell silent, staring, weaving a little, as though remembering being a tree and shaken by a mild-tempered breeze. And then he laughed.

"Wasn't that dumb?" he grinned.

Billy grinned back and was happy, because everything was all right again. Father had fixed it; and then his father inhaled deeply. And he smiled down at his son, with eyes sparkling brightly until they seemed to trip over something that gradually swam into his line of vision and he had to refocus.

Reorienting himself, he sighed deeply, smacked his lips once or twice and then squatted beside his son, lurching a little to maintain his balance. He pointed to the highway where busy little cars were still rushing towards the city.

"Look at them!" he shouted, his voice dropping to a heavy whisper.

"The poor, sad people. They never knew what it was to be a tree. Just keep rushing to the dark, buried city. And trees never grow there. Not real ones. Not big ones. But they don't know that. Or maybe they just forgot." He looked down at the earth between his feet, and his head started to weave.

"The city's a terrible place, Billy. Especially on a Saturday. People get lost in the city. Never come out. And never know that it's Saturday. And they never know how green fields can get. Never know what it's like to be growing."

His father was a miracle, Billy thought. He had been a tree and grown from the same earth that other men only walked on. He lived close to so many simple and wonderful things, dreaming fairy tales that came alive. Things like—

"The unicorn," Billy said.

"Yes. The unicorn...Never forget about him, hear? Look everyplace and always believe or it'll never come to you. Then you'll be an old man all your life. Your mother's going to tell you that you'll never see it. She's even said that I've never seen it. But I really have...honest, cross my heart...But you can't blame her, you know. She's just a grownup. She's not a kid, not like you and me."

He was staring out towards the highway, but he was looking beyond the cars, towards somewhere over the crest of a rounded hill, swelling out of a large stand of trees.

"That's one of the troubles of becoming a grownup. That's why I never want to be older than you are. When you're a grownup, you don't have anything left to believe. You sort of change things around to something else. You know, like you might swap somebody a knife for some marbles. One of your friends, maybe. Only when you get home, you find all the marbles cracked or something. It's like that. You really think you want what you're getting, but you learn later that what you gave away is really what you wanted all the time."

His eyes strayed from the hill and came to rest on the house. Their house. His hand patted the bulging pocket.

"Enough talk, Billy," Father said, rising to his feet. "Let's go into the woods. We'll never give away the woods, eh?"

They tramped across the glowing field, a field vibrant and alive with the sun. The tall grass and weeds swished and parted for them, releasing swarms of light, tickling bugs. A wasp buzzed around his father's ear and he let out a bellow of make-believe panic and blundered through the grass in a crashing, awkward flight. Billy laughed up towards the sun and then ran after him. He waited for him, and together they watched a white butterfly dance its ballet through the sunlight. Billy suddenly wanted to shout as his father had shouted, and race with the breeze for the shadows of the secret forest. But he held the scream inside him as he watched the butterfly's dance with wonder.

Billy looked around him, and suddenly realized that they were deep in the woods, wrapped in the solemn dignity of subdued and reverent light. Whispers were needed here because here there were deep mysteries, of life and growth. And like the trees, Billy knew that he—Billy Wilson—was growing, too. And he was growing always, for yesterday's Billy Wilson was no longer today's Billy Wilson, and by tomorrow he might grow to be like the towering man striding through the gold-flecked light beside him.

The woods became of long ago, the silent forests of stalking Indians, a humming, shimmering world of trees existing with no need for human eyes or ears. Strange, dark trees were all around him, hiding mysteries not intended for the sight of little boys. It would be here, he thought, and soon. Because each moment had lead to another moment that could only be leading to another particular moment. He listened carefully. He watched. But nothing happened.

His father sat down heavily at the foot of a tree and leaned his head back. "Go on by yourself for a while, son," he sighed. "I'll catch up."

Billy went on, excitement pounding in his chest. Looking back to make certain he wasn't being followed, he saw his father take a long swallow from a bottle he'd pulled from his pocket.

The woods closed around Billy, and he was alone. A million miles alone. A million years. He believed the unicorn would come to him. He realized that he didn't really believe before, but he needed to believe for it to come. And he believed everything now: the single leaf that remained quiet in the midst of an excited tree, the golden daylight that stretched and pulled itself into night. Everything was here and there could be no secrets.

He walked carefully, attentively. Ahead was a low clump of brush and there was something in back, moving slightly to stir the branches. He poked his head through the brush.

The forest offered a creature of spotted brown, with jaws moving reflectively and big, brown eyes. The sight of a boy's head was a strange one, and sufficiently puzzling to be avoided. And so the shy creature turned and moved primly deeper into the privacy of the forest. But the boy saw magic, and a twisty horn growing from the head. And the color was lavender.

He had seen it, and his heart knew that it was true and just the way he saw it. And the forest crackled and snapped as the magic creature pushed through the underbrush.

He could run after it, Billy thought. He could see it again. But he knew it was just as he saw it. Why make a lie out of Saturday? Why doubt and never see it again?

He turned and ran back to his father.

His father was where he had left him, an empty bottle resting in his limp hand. Father's head bobbed and wobbled, and he smiled vacantly at the air. Billy touched him on the shoulder, and Father looked up and stared at him for a long time. And then the man laughed, joyously, breaking the silence. But Billy didn't want to hear the laughter and he felt ashamed, because everything here was holy, and he wanted to hear everything growing.

"Billy, my son!" his father shouted. "My little Pan! Did you dance and sing? Did you see everything? Did you listen to the trees talk?"

Billy's father reeked from a strong, sticky smell, and he looked different. He looked old and soft, and didn't seem to belong in the same woods with lavender unicorns. He didn't look like someone who had ever been a tree; he seemed to be lying on the ground like an old soft worm, eating away at the vision of the unicorn.

"I saw it," Bill said quietly, trying to save the moment. "The unicorn. In the woods. Like the apron."

His father nodded his head vigorously. "Sure you did," he said. "Sure. I know. You're my son, aren't you? And I saw him, too. More than one. They come when I call and leave when I say so. Flocks of them—bevies of them."

Billy's father laughed to himself, muttering hoarsely. And then he laughed again.

It was ending the way it always did on those certain days. Mother would be angry, Billy thought, and there would be shouting. And Mother would come to his room and squeeze him and hold him until he felt sick, and would whisper things to him that he wouldn't understand. But he didn't care about that, because something else was happening. The unicorn was changing, the color was fading into something else. All the magic was leaving him; Billy tried his best to stop it, but he couldn't. He saw again the magic creature moving into the woods, and heard the snapping branches and the rustling of leaves. And then Saturday was suddenly over, an old, tired day eager for the deadness of night. And it seemed to him that he would be an old man forever.

"Home," he said to his father.

"Yes, home. Mother will be waiting. The screens have to be up. Lots of other things, too. Let's do a lot of work around the house, eh? Make Mother proud of us. Show her what good workers we are."

It took a long time to get home, with his father staggering and almost falling a few times. Mother was waiting for them at the door. Her face and lips grew tight when she saw them. Father stopped before her, smiling like a little boy.

"I'll put them up," he said. "But don't...don't...."

Then he laughed loudly in her face. A roaring laugh, doubling him up, bringing tears to his eyes.

"Go upstairs, Billy," said Mother. "Right now. Your father and I want to talk."

Trembling, he went, returning to the warm privacy of his bed. Even before the daylight died, the little room was invaded by the dark, creeping things of night, and Billy Wilson felt like a frightened old man.

Children Are Monsters

BILL JAMIESON STRAIGHTENED UP carefully, testing his stiff back. It creaked a little, so he held his breath until he was upright, and then released it in a long, groaning sigh. He leaned on the handle of the rake and ruefully inspected his blistered, sore hands. He'd never seen his hands in that condition. He wrinkled his nose in disgust and turned to see what all those blisters had accomplished.

Nothing, he told himself. Absolutely nothing. Looks just as bad as when I started.

The barren, unsodded yard crested and fell in waves towards the back. A low spot sank in one corner and a high spot rose in another, and in between the ground was lumpy and filled with large, stubborn rocks. It looked like that when he'd started; after two hours, it hadn't changed. All he'd succeeded in doing was raising lots of dust and mussing up his hair. He ran the palms of his hands over his temples, and tried to coax a few perverse strands away from his face, and into their proper place. But it was useless; they sprang out again and clung wetly to his forehead.

Why doesn't someone write a book, he thought, to prepare novice home owners for the labor and nuisance that acquiring a new house involves? Books have been written on everything else—why not on the business of owning a home? It would seem a very useful thing. There could be a whole chapter—maybe an entire volume—on how to level a backyard.

He grunted fretfully and stared unhappily at the ground, perspiration rolling down his neck. He grimaced, not liking to sweat, and reached for his handkerchief. It was very dirty but he was past caring. He looked up at the sky and sighed. It looked gray and somber, and a touch of approaching night was chilling the air.

It was late August. The days were getting shorter and September was on the way. Children would be starting for school soon, and the Jamiesons' vacation would be over.

Bill's wife, Alice, waved to him from the kitchen window. She held a scrubbing brush in her hand and made a wry face at it. Bill smiled wanly at her as she left the window and returned to the inside work.

He liked Alice; better than that, respected her. She was a small, pretty woman, energetic and good-humored, with soft brown hair and a brain that was usually quite practical. He considered himself very lucky, and never once thought of his pleasant bachelor days. In fact, he would never have remembered them, except for the house.

Why, he asked himself for the upteenth time, why did she want a house? The apartment had been perfect. They'd have to search months to find one like that again. No yard, no lawn. And no heating bills, no electric bills, no gas bills. What in the world did they need with a house?

And what pained him the most was having to cut their vacation short, simply to work on the damn thing. He almost moaned on recalling the beautiful cottage they'd rented that summer. On a deep, cool lake that was home to thousands of cooperative and utterly stupid fish. Far from any settlements, they were surrounded by a green, murmurous forest, where he could read whatever he wanted, smoke a calm pipe in the peace and quiet, and dream in front of a glowing fireplace.

Then they came back to their gawky, new house in their gawky, new neighborhood, raw with upturned, rocky earth, and treeless for miles in all directions.

Farther down the block, a baby started to cry. Soon, four or five older children began screaming at the top of their lungs. And the children! Hordes of them, spilling out of every house, screaming under every window. Bill threw his head back, and appealed to the heavens.

He stretched his back a little and looked down at the rake, considering another joust with the yard. Instead, he leaned on it and wrinkled his nose, sighing deeply.

It was the children, most of all, that bothered him, he thought. And it was another point for the apartment. Very wisely, families with children were barred from the building. They had to live someplace, it was true. But surely, people had the right to expect peace and quiet after a hard day of teaching.

He stared abstractly at nothing.

What was it made children so difficult to civilize, he wondered? Left to themselves, they invariably acted like little savages. Only the presence of adults could prevent revolution. At least until they learned to defy the adults. Like that little monster the other morning. Bill shuddered, thinking about that first morning.

*****

THEY WERE SLEEPING *a little late after the first night in the new house. It had taken them a while to fall asleep. What with the smell of fresh paint and new wood, and the creaking night noises around and in the house, they lay awake most of the night. Bill especially had a difficult time. He always found it trying the first night in a strange room.*

So he lay half-awake, content and lazy in the wide bed, listening to the sounds of day outside: sparrows quarreling, an occasional car passing on the street in front. He smiled contentedly, telling himself that it might not be too bad owning a home, and started to sink back into sleep.

"Get that shotgun back in the house!" someone roared.

Bill sprang out of bed, wide awake, eyes staring. He trembled a little, he almost cringed.

"What's the matter, Bill?" Alice asked sleepily.

"Someone's got a gun in back," he whispered shakily.

"Clarence, bring it back!" the voice roared again.

"Clarence?" Bill whispered.

"Come and get it if you want it," a boys voice answered.

He's going to shoot it out, Bill thought.

"Come back to bed," Alice said. "You're dreaming again." She rolled over on her side.

"Dreaming!" he protested. "Could I be dreaming that uproar?"

She mumbled something he couldn't understand, and then was silent. Bill tried prodding her, but she stubbornly refused to be awakened. He felt very lonely.

He sat on the edge of the bed, but couldn't force himself to lie down. He considered stealing into the kitchen and spying through the windows, but dismissed the thought as dangerous, So he just sat, shivering a little because his feet were getting cold.

My God, he wondered, how many children are like that? And he shuddered for the future of his country.

*****

BACK IN THE present, Bill shook his head slowly and made some dispirited little jabs at the ground with his rake. What are the kids at school going to be like this year, he wondered? What plots concocted behind those sweet, innocent faces? He took a deep breath, hefted the rake a few times and hurled himself at the yard.

He hacked the ground doggedly for several minutes. When the door slammed next door, he glanced up and noticed that the neighbor's child, a little girl of five or six, had come into the yard. She seemed a quiet, well-behaved little girl from what he'd seen of her, but he zeroed in on a large, half buried rock that seemed determined to resist his efforts at excavation, and forgot all about her.

The little girl climbed up on the fence her father had built during the summer. She watched Bill solemnly for a number of minutes.

"H'lo Mr. Jamieson," she said finally.

Bill returned the salutation without pause in his labors. But the little girl was curious and wanted his full attention.

"Wha'cha doin'?" she wanted to know.

With that, Bill stopped, leaned on the rake and looked at his small interrogator. She was a gentle-looking girl with big, solemn eyes and a wistful little mouth.

"I'm raking," Bill answered.

"Oh," the little girl said, her brow wrinkling as she puzzled over Bill's answer.

Bill prepared himself for the return to his battle with the yard, when the little girl thought of something else.

"My daddy finished raking long ago," she informed him.

Bill stopped abruptly and threw an agonized look up at the sky. Even the sweet looking ones, he muttered to himself.

Even the little angels have an infallible instinct for saying exactly the wrong thing.

He was busy thinking up a killing riposte to the little girl's comment when her mother came to the back door and called her.

"Come here a minute Nora," she called. "Hello there, Bill. Still working I see."

Bill checked the impulse to ask how the devil she could be so astute, but could think of nothing else to say, so he just nodded and smiled. Pleasantly, he hoped.

"Come here, Nora," the woman said.

"I'm visiting with Mr. Jamieson."

"Well, I'm sure he'll excuse you," her mother answered smiling brightly at Bill while he murmured a fervent amen. "I want you to take care of your little brother for a few minutes."

The little girl hopped down from the fence and skipped to the back door where she collected her year-old brother and led him out into the yard. The baby toddled a few steps, then squatted suddenly to keep from falling down. While there, the little boy apparently decided to inspect the quality of the grass.

"Take good care of him now," the mother said, popping back into the house.

Bill watched the kid diligently tearing up handfuls of sod. His sister kneeled in front of him, a look of intense concentration on her face.

Bill returned to his rake, grateful for the break from his little visitor, but discreetly watching the two. He saw the little girl glance quickly toward the kitchen window, then throw a sly look towards Bill. Thinking herself unobserved, a vengeful look filled her face and she slapped her baby brother hard , shoving him over as he screamed in shock and pain. The mother burst out of the house, into the yard and picked up the screaming child.

"What happened?" she wanted to know, rocking the baby in her arms.

"He fell down, Mama. Poor baby. And I couldn't even catch him because he fell down so hard."

The mother crooned to her baby, still rocking him as his screams continued. She walked into the house with him, followed closely by the concerned big sister, who wore a look of anguished concern on her sweet little face.

The angel-faced little monster, thought Bill, sharing the baby's shocked surprise. How can you tell what goes on behind those dewy little eyes? What dark things lie there?

He shook his head slowly, thinking that although he'd taught them for so many years, he'd never known, never really known any of them. They were always partly in shadows, parts of them hidden and unknowable, except for brief instances when the shadowed part strode into the light. And then, they could change into something dark and alien. Like the one all 'A' student last year, who spent much of his free time after school working in the chemistry lab. He was the prize student, the one teachers held up as a model when admonishing the lesser minds in the class. He'd even adopted Bill as his confidential counselor, which made Bill very proud. Students didn't usually confide in him. Most of them thought him pompous and dull, and enjoyed playing jokes on him to destroy his composure. Until this one, and this one was a prize. One such student every ten years, Bill had thought, was reward enough for the penny-pinching life of a school teacher. But one day, talking with the boy, Bill learned—and quite casually, now that he thought of it—the boy was designing a bomb to blow up the school. Bill would have laughed, except for the glint of madness he saw in the boy's eyes. Even when the boy snickered, he was sure that it was no joke. And the jeering amusement in the eyes of the other students told him that they knew of the boy's plan and all silently approved.

It's a plot, he thought. No one can convince me it was a joke. Not with that look in his eyes. A plot to exterminate the entire adult population!

Bill thought back to what his first principal had told him when he started teaching. The principal, a childless man himself, had a big nose with a wart on the tip, a soft white, face and a small mouth that looked as though it had tasted something disagreeable early in life and never recovered. Bill recalled that his voice sounded weak and femininely musical.

"They're demons!" the man had said. "Revolutionists. All of them, without exception. They're just waiting for everyone to turn their backs at the same time so they can spring and take over the world, unhampered by laws and conventions. You've got to watch them constantly. Slacken your hold on them at your own peril."

He was right, Bill thought. If only they were born old enough to vote.

Alice was standing at the back door calling to him.

"Hey, Farmer Bill," she called. "You ready to call it a day?"

"I was ready to call it a day two hours ago," he smiled. "Come out and see what I've accomplished."

She walked into the yard towards Bill, looking about her as she came. Pausing next to him, she took a long look around the yard.

"What?" she wanted to know; Bill chuckled darkly.

"Precisely what I've been asking since I started this silly business."

She patted him fondly on the shoulder.

"Don't worry. Eventually we'll be finished. And then we can just sit back and enjoy our home.

"I doubt that," Bill replied. "I doubt that very much. I think we've sold ourselves into a life of eternal toil. We've placed ourselves in bondage to what the builder, probably laughingly, referred to as a 'moderately-priced home'."

"Are you sorry?" Alice asked ruefully.

"I suppose not. Not really, anyhow. I just keep thinking of our comfortable, care-free life in that apartment. No bills, no lawns, no children. By the way—have you noticed the army of children that surround us?"

Alice gave him a peculiar look before replying. Bill's heart skipped a beat because it looked so much like the look children have, just before they reveal the fiendish side of their nature.

"There do seem to be quite a few," she answered in a rather cautious voice. "Do they bother you?"

"No...not really," he answered uneasily.

Disconcerted by the look in her eyes, he changed the subject. Peering up at the sky he remarked on the quickening of dusk.

"Days are getting shorter," Alice sighed. "Summer is almost over. Such a nice summer too, It's sad seeing it go."

"Back to school," he sighed. "I just hope I don't have that pimply-face kid, Albert again. With those pictures he always carries with him."

"Oh, they're all pretty nice kids when you get to know them."

"I know them! They're monsters."

She gave him that strange look again.

"Well, I'm going in," she said, moving away. "There's still the kitchen floor to do." At the door, she remembered something and turned towards Bill.

"By the way," she said, 'the paper boy will be by for his money. Would you pay him? I told him you'd be in the backyard. Have you met him?"

Bill shook his head.

"A real sweet little boy," she said dreamily. "Fiery red hair and freckles all over his face. He lives right in back of us."

"I'll take care of it."

She nodded her head absently and went into the house. Bill stared at the closed door uneasily, There was something oddly soft and weepy about the way she was acting. It was making him feel awkward and lonely, as though she had suddenly turned into a stranger. He flayed the ground with the rake another time, hoping to drive some ridiculous notions out of his mind.

He was just finishing and ready to throw down the rake, when the paper boy came whistling up the walk along the side of the house. He came around the corner and grinned broadly at Bill. The boy had an infectious grin, so Bill grinned back.

The boy's hair was like fire, and his sparkling eyes smiled happily from an alert young face. A friendly boy, Bill thought. Nothing secret or dark about him.

"Hi, Mr. Jamieson," the boy said cheerfully. "I'm Jimmy Kendall, your paper boy."

Bill straightened up, rocked on his heels a little as he did when lecturing a class, and smiled brightly down at the little boy.

"Hello Jimmy," he said heartily. "Nice meeting you."

He dug into his pocket and fished out a dollar.

"Eighty-five cents, isn't it? Here...take this and keep the change."

"Gee, thanks!"

Bill felt himself warming to the boy, and regretted not giving him a bigger tip. "What grade are you in school, Jimmy?" he asked, clasping his hands behind his back.

"Sixth."

"Sixth!" Bill exclaimed with a show of astonishment as he rocked up on his toes. "Why, that's fine! Just fine! And I'll bet you like school, don't you? Can't wait to get back, eh?"

"Oh, I guess so. I was in trouble with some teachers last year. But I won't be this year, I think."

Bill chuckled indulgently. "You shouldn't have trouble with teachers," he said. "They're nice people, I'm a teacher, you know."

"You are?"

The boy looked at him with new interest. A calculating look came into his eyes.

"You teach chemistry?" the boy asked.

Bill sucked in his breath sharply. "Why, no," he laughed hollowly. "I teach history."

"I like to learn about chemistry. It's fun. My older brother goes to high school and he tells me about it sometime. I've got a chemistry set in the garage." And he pointed to the ramshackle building in back. With a sinking feeling in his stomach, Bill noticed that all the glass had been broken out of the windows.

"That's very nice," Bill said unsteadily, started to back away towards the house. "I've got to go Billy. It's been nice talking with you. We'll do it again, sometime."

"Mr. Jamieson," the boy called after him. "Did you ever study chemistry?"

Bill quivered and turned around.

"Just a little," he said shakily. "But that was a long time ago."

The boy moved closer to him and stared up into his eyes. Bill stared down as though hypnotized.

"Mr. Jamieson," the boy asked softly, "do you know anything about uranium?"

Goodnight, Father

THE LAST HOURS OF A workday afternoon were the longest, especially when the days turned misty. Looking down from the fifth floor, the trees were empty and black, and they didn't soften the city the way they could when they were new with Spring. I'd get sullen and sleepy and look for excuses to leave early. So, as Mr. Roy Mack's administrative assistant, I decided that I ought to pay a visit to one of his sales analysts, who'd been hospitalized with some sort of physical breakdown.

I walked down to Roy's office in the air conditioned wing. Fran, his secretary, was typing something. She worked with the intense, strained urgency that seemed the posture of anyone who worked for Mack.

"Is he in?" I asked.

"Yes, yes," she said. Her neck was thin and stretched over the typewriter. The furniture in this outer office was richly brown and modern; the chairs looked comfortable, but Fran never did.

"Well, can I see him?"

She looked up, startled. Tentatively, as though hoping I'd change my mind, she reached for the phone. She paused a moment for a deep breath, before pushing a button and holding the phone gingerly to her ear.

After a moment, she flinched and started to speak. Then she stopped, cleared her throat, and started again.

"Wally—I beg your pardon, sir—but Wally would like to talk to you." She listened diligently, nodding her head. She looked up at me.

"Is it important?" she asked.

"Not really. Tell him I thought I'd visit Bill at the hospital."

She repeated what I'd said into the phone and listened again, very carefully. Then she put down the phone and released her breath in a long, shuddering sigh.

"He wants to see you before you go." She passed her hand across her forehead and seemed surprised at the perspiration. I smiled pleasantly and went inside.

Roy Mack's office was big and brown and quiet. As Merchandising and Product Manager for the Hansen Motor Company, he was entitled to a three-window office, plus a home in Bloomfield Hills, a membership at Oakland Hills, and an expensively chromed company car. The three big windows were hidden behind the heavy beige drapes. Along the wall, two bookcases were filled with binders of statistics, and engineering reports. There were five chairs and a couch. In front of the couch was a long, low table with some motor magazines on it, and a gold cigarette box.

He was a tall, tight man with thinning hair over a high forehead. His eyes were cold behind rimless glasses, and a muscle in his jaw pumped continuously like a machine. On his desk was a desk pen set, with three pens slanting out of a heavy gold base. There were also three matching ashtrays and a lighter. On the table behind him was a small golf trophy, and a framed picture of his little boy.

"You're going to look in on Bill?"

I nodded.

"Sit down for a minute. I need to make a call and then I want you to do something for me."

I sat down and listened to him get Fran unhinged again, asking her to get someone for him at Engineering. It was his voice that did it to people. It was high-pitched and shrill, a stranger to whispers, and it seemed to trigger everyone's nerve endings, making them sit up and beg.

"Where is he, Fran?" he demanded into the phone. "Are we playing some sort of game here?" His voice was high and taut, vibrating like an E-string. It was especially effective when asking rhetorical questions.

He listened to Fran's answer and them smiled coldly.

"I didn't ask you to find out where he's gone, Fran," he said tightly. "Maybe you didn't understand me? I said I wanted to talk to him on the phone. Now, that's not an unreasonable request, is it? I didn't ask you to find out if he's attending a meeting. What I *did* ask you to do—at the risk of repeating myself—was to get him on the phone for me. Is that clear now? Do you understand now? Do you think you could do that for me?"

My eyes drifted to the picture of his boy. The lad was about eight—a pale little boy with big eyes and an unsmiling mouth, dressed in some sort of fussy party suit. I'd never met him, but I'd talked to him often on the phone. Mack rarely got home in time to tuck him in bed, but he always called at bedtime to say goodnight. Unless, of course, he was tied up with something important. Then he'd have me do it. Sometimes I wondered whether, in my capacity as his administrative aide, one evening I might be called on to administer to his wife's needs.

"Fran, I've wasted enough time on this damn phone," he said. "You keep at it and get him on here as soon as you can. Hear?"

He slammed the phone down and cursed it.

"So help me, Wally," he said, "I'm going to get rid of that skinny bitch."

"Let up on her," I said. "She's wound up so tight now she's liable to snap. You've already got one guy in the hospital. Stop trying for two."

"What the hell do you mean?"

"You know damn well that Bill was going full throttle, eighteen hours a day for a solid month before he finally blew a gasket. You keep it up the way you are and Fran will blow, too. Might make you look bad."

"Yeah, yeah," he glared at me. He picked up a pencil and started chewing it. He seemed to forget about me for a while, before he finally remembered what he'd wanted.

"When you go to see Bill, do something for me."

"Sure."

"Saturday's my boy's birthday," he said. "And I won't be home until late. Get something for him from me and send it out to the house. Go to Saks. They can charge my account."

I thought of the pale, ghostlike little boy with big eyes and the tiny faded voice.

"Get something for him? Like what?"

"Hell, I don't know! You've got kids. You should know what kids like."

"Mine like baseball. Does yours?"

"I don't know. But he could learn, couldn't he?"

"Maybe a construction set. Does he like to build things?"

"He could learn! Anything you get, he could learn to use, couldn't he?"

"Yeah, I guess so. Kids learn easy."

As I left, Fran was still holding tight to the phone. She needed fresh lipstick, and her eyes were red.

So it was October and wet and I was going to visit a sick man because it got me out of work early. And now I had to buy a present for a tiny, disembodied voice.

*****

THE HOSPITAL WAS old and sweaty and damp. It was on a street that was called a boulevard but the island that would have made it into one was gone, swallowed by the widened street. Big old houses edged the street; once warmed by the pulse of a home, they'd been taken over by the musty needs of musty little businesses: photographers, ad men, con men, musty men.

A skinny tree stood in front of the hospital on a sliver of brown lawn. Two sparrows, fat against the wet chill, sat on a shiny black branch and swore dispiritedly at one another. Occasionally, they'd find fault with the people walking past them towards the hospital.

What the hell was I doing here, I wondered. I followed a huge woman into the hospital, one with enormously thick ankles. She took the elevator. I took the stairs.

The hum of visiting hours warmed the cold white corridors. The click of heels muffled the squeal of white shoes on tile. Laughter hid the scratchy sounds of white starch. Even the medicine smell was diluted by the aromas coming from the lounge at the end of the corridor. There was a crowd around the TV set, and I remembered it was World Series time. Pirates against the Yankees.

I walked into Bill's room, wondering again why I was here. I really didn't like him. His laugh always followed Mack's too closely; his eyes followed Mack's suggestions too enthusiastically. He started when I entered, and kept looking in back of me to see if someone else was following.

"Well, Bill," I said heartily, eyes suffused with manly solicitude, I was sure, "how's it going, boy?"

"Oh, fine, fine," he said, eyes on the move, a smile coming and going automatically, flickering steadily like a neon sign.

"Mack wanted me to see how you were going."

"Tell him fine. Tell him I'll be back before he knows it. And tell him thanks for asking. Tell him thanks."

There were two beds in the room. Bill's was next to the window. It was the second floor along the front; the tree was down below, but the sparrows had gone someplace else. The other bed was rumpled. There were newspapers on it, as well as a hat and coat.

"Where's the roommate?"

"Watching television in the lounge, I guess. He's a nut about baseball." His fingers plucked and plucked at the edging of the blanket.

"Young guy?"

"No, old. Talks with an accent. Look about Mack...you will tell him that I'll be back soon?"

"I'll tell him. Don't worry, I'll tell him." I was sneaking a look at my watch and wondering how soon I could leave when two men walked in.

The old man was short and round and chesty. He was wearing an old flannel robe over his hospital gown. The slippers he wore slapped the floor whenever he took a step, and his legs, showing beneath the gown when he sat on the edge of the bed, were stumpy and bowed. He was dark, with a scratchy-looking chin and fierce eyes. His mouth and chin were stubborn, and his hands were dirty-looking around the nails, his fingers half-curled as if remembering a tool.

The younger man was taller, thinner and not as dark. He looked like a son, and a harried one at that. He was maybe thirty years old, dressed in a well-tailored flannel suit and shiny black shoes. His hair was cropped close and his fingers were long and white.

The old man didn't notice me at first. The son did and nodded pleasantly.

The father talked with a heavy, East European accent, and was telling his son that maybe he should go back to work pretty darn quick because why stay here when nothing is doing and could be he'd lose his job and then who-the-hell would support him? But before he did that, he shouldn't forget about all he'd been told. About taking all the nuts and bolts from the basement. About all that good, almost unused lumber in the garage. About all the tools and vises and the ladders he should take. But most of all—most of all, the power saw. With plenty of attachments and no more payments at Sears.

Every half sentence or so, he'd thrown in a "don' forget now!" but from the look he'd give his son, it was obvious that he knew damn well the young idiot would forget everything as soon as he left. Throughout the long inventory, the son tried to interrupt once or twice, but in the end gave up and just nodded his head whenever a nod seemed called for.

"All right, now you go," the old man said.

"You sure, now?" the son asked.

"Yeah, I'm sure now."

A quiet flicker of emotion passed between them. It was over in a heartbeat, and they grinned at one another. The son put his arms around his father's neck and kissed him on the bristled cheek, and the father kissed him back. Then, as the son picked up his coat and hat, the old man finally noticed me.

"Hey, hello!" he called. "You maybe drive here?"

I told him that I had.

"How you gon' back?"

"Now, Pa," the son protested.

"Never mind now. If he gon' your way, he no mind it."

I told them I would be going near the Fisher Building and if it was on the way, I'd be glad to oblige them.

"See!" the old man said gleefully.

The son grinned at me and shook his head. "Are you sure you don't mind?" he asked. And I told him no.

"Now you save taxi fare, eh?" the father pointed out. The old man looked at Bill now who was lying very still, staring up at the ceiling with his fingers still working at the blanket.

"How your friend?" he asked.

"Better, I guess."

"I think maybe he worry about job. You his foreman?"

"No, I'm not his foreman. And he doesn't have to worry. His boss told me."

"That's fine. I live in the Depression. It does something bad to a man who has to worry about job." He got broody for a moment, so I thought I'd cheer him up.

"How's the Series going?" I asked.

He perked up and thought about the question. He shrugged his shoulder, cocked his head, and drew down the corners of his mouth. "Those Pirates look like nice young team. But those Yankees! Awful goddamn lucky. And too much publicity."

"They're pretty good besides."

He glanced at me sharply.

"You follow the Yankees?" he asked gruffly.

"No sir. I'm a Tiger fan all the way."

"Then they are lucky!" he roared good-naturedly. He folded his arms and tried to cross his legs but couldn't manage the hospital gown they'd put him in.

"Why you can' wear pants here I don' know," he complained to himself.

"Okay," he smiled at his son, "you go speak gentle to Mama. And don' worry," he said to me, "I take care of your friend." He escorted his son out the door, apparently not wishing to intrude on my own goodbyes, so I hurried to say goodbye to Bill.

"Don't forget to tell Mack," he said and his face started to work. I nodded and left quickly, afraid that he was going to start crying.

I caught up with the father and son at the head of the stairs. The father was going through the inventory one more time. As we reached the main floor, he was back to the power saw again. The son and I were on the floor level; the father was a stair or two above us.

"That power saw—with attachments—I want you should have. Go to house and take it tonight. You can do everything with it. You should have it. I want you should have it."

"Pa, you know how I am with tools. I call an electrician to change a light bulb. And this power saw you want me to have. I'll just ruin it or lop off a finger or something. I just don't know how to use it."

The old man's face darkened and he seemed to swell and grow bigger with his anger. His eagle-like eyes grew fierce; it was like watching a storm gathering in the sky.

"Well, you could learn!" he thundered, and began walking back up the staircase. Half way up, he turned and glared down at his son.

"*You could learn!*" he roared. He turned and stormed up the stairs. In the calm that followed, the son and I looked at one another.

"By George," I said at last, "there's a man who means to be heard."

The son grinned wryly at me and shrugged his shoulders, the same way his father had. "That's my Pop," he said, looking up the empty staircase.

Later, in the car, I asked him about the list of stuff his father kept rattling off at him.

"I guess you'd call it my legacy," he said and studied his hands for a minute. "He's got cancer." He looked out the window. "You know," he continued, "I wish the hell I knew how to use that stuff."

The mist had turned into a slight drizzle, and the wiper blades beat out a gentle rhythm. Outside, lonely trees passed, black and empty.

"By the way," he asked, "you sure this isn't out of your way? Pop can sometimes get people doing things they never really wanted to do."

"No. I've got to buy a gift for someone at Saks."

And then, I was going home to kiss my two boys.

Mary

THE MASS WAS VERY NICE. The priest said nice things about Stanley Janik. All his friends were there. Some of them had come from Pennsylvania where Stanley had met and married Sophie Kularski. They all looked very old.

Mrs. Sophie Janik rode in the car with her daughter and son-in-law. She was a very frail-looking woman of sixty with the bone structure of a bird. Her eyes squinted behind thick glasses and she carried her head thrust forward as though trying to get closer to whatever she was looking at. Her lips were very thin and severe. Helen, her daughter, was a dishwater blond and big-boned. Helen's hair was drawn straight back and gathered in a bun at the nape of the neck. Her eyes were dark and glowing, but her lips had assumed the severe lines of her mother. Her husband, Max Nemski, was a big, fleshy man with a round flushed face and thinning hair. There were fine red lines traced in the white of his slightly popped eyes. He and Helen were both in their mid-thirties.

"The two plots were very nice, Mama," Helen said.

The plots were on the side of a hill near two small trees. The trees were small now, but someday they would be very big.

"They are very nice," the mother said in Polish. "Just what he would have liked. And we saved money by getting two plots."

Max snorted and his wife poked at him viciously, glaring at him, her lips tight and pale.

"Can't you see I'm driving," he snapped. "Lay off when I'm driving."

It was a wet, windy day and the ground had been wet and heavy, turning to yellow, sticky mud.

"Later on there will be plenty of sun and sky," Mrs. Janik mused, unaware of the slight squabble that had gone on over her head. "From the hill you can see the crowded streets and past them, the airport. On nice days, the small planes will fly right over the hill. They are like little toys. So strange that people will fly in something so small." She sighed and pursed her lips. "They must be very expensive." All her life, she had worried about money and expenses. Auto plants shut down so often, she always had to plan for the lean times.

MAX STARED TO drink as soon as they got to the house. And every time someone else came in, he insisted on taking the men out through the kitchen where the women were cooking, down the stairs into the basement where the beer and whiskey was set up. He already looked sweaty and rumpled, and his eyes blinked very slowly. Mrs. Janik told Helen to say something to him. But he only swore when she did. Mrs. Janik sat down stiffly in the red mohair chair in the living room that faced the front door.

It was a small frame house on Detroit's east side with a whisper of space between it and its neighbors. It was so small that more than ten people seemed like a crowd. It got even smaller when a huge man walked through the front doorway. "Sophie Janik!" he roared. He spread his arms wide and stepped back, bumping into the front wall. A picture of the Virgin Mary was knocked awry, exposing a piece of chipped wall that Stanley Janik had never gotten around to fixing. The man straightened the picture and smiling broadly came to Mrs. Janik. His shoes were covered with yellow mud and he tracked some of it on the rug.

"Peter Yaros," said Mrs. Janik. "I did not see you at the church or the cemetery."

"I was at the cemetery, but you were already gone. Was it a nice funeral?"

"There were twenty-five cars," she answered proudly. "That is very good for a weekday."

He was fat. She had always said he would be fat, Mrs. Janik remembered as she looked up at the fleshy red face bulging out of the sweaty, crumpled shirt collar. Even when they were young in Pennsylvania and Peter was a powerful, bellowing miner who could best anyone in town, she'd said he would end up a fat old man. She had even told him that to his face, she thought, the times when he'd carried Stanley, sick with drink, into their bedroom.

"But it is nice to see you again, Missus!" he bellowed in Polish. His belly bulged, straining at the shirt buttons, and somewhere underneath the bulge, his belt buckle was buried out of sight. "It has been such a long, long time." His pants were all wrinkled and stained, and there was yellow mud along the edge of the cuffs. "We used to be such good friends, your Stanley and me. Remember? Ah! How mad you would get at us!" He roared with laughter, the mass of him shaking. His hair used to be black and curly, she remembered, and all the young girls loved to hear him sing the Old Country songs. Now the light shone where the hair had been, and the voice wheezed with the fat. "I am so sorry about Stanley. But I am glad I could come."

"How did you get here, Peter?"

"I flew."

Over the hills and the trees, from the coal fields to Detroit. How strange it was.

"It must have been very expensive."

"My son paid for it. He is a doctor." He grinned sheepishly.

"How nice that he was a doctor," Mrs. Janik said, thinking of the poor dead thing she had borne. He could have been a doctor. She remembered how Stanley had cried. As though his hurt could have been any greater than hers.

She asked for her daughter, who was in the dining room setting up the table for the food, to get Max. He and Peter would get along, she thought. Helen asked one of the ladies in the kitchen to call for her husband. After a moment, he thumped up the stairs, stumbling once.

When he came through the kitchen door, he almost bumped into the dining room table that had been pushed from the center of the room to the outside wall. Helen whispered furiously at him and he told her to get off his back.

"This is Mr. Yaros, Max," Mrs. Janik said. "Maybe he would like something."

The two big men grinned at one another, enjoying each other's gluttonous bulk.

"Mr. Yaros," Max said, "you look like you need a drink, and then something to eat. Hah? You shouldn't go back home looking quite so skinny."

Peter Yaros roared with laughter and hugged the younger man. Laughing, the two men moved cautiously through the dining room toward the kitchen. They had to stop there as four or five of the ladies passed through the door carrying trays of food. Mr. Yaros sniffed appreciatively and made loud smacking sounds. There were steaming platters of red moist kielbasa, stuffed cabbage and Polish-style sauerkraut, potato dumplings, and jars of home-canned hot peppers and green tomatoes.

While he was waiting, Peter thought of something.

"Remember Mary Ryan, Missus?" he called back.

"Yes, I think so. She was in the house next to the tracks?"

"Yes, yes. She was that one. Dark little girl with big eyes."

She remembered; how well she remembered. Sophie Janik had been an old married woman of twenty-one, worrying about groceries, bills, and her husband. Mary Ryan remained the laughing, young girl with big eyes up until the time Sophie and her husband had left for Detroit. She was dead now.

"Oh, yes," she said. "I remember now."

"How long ago it was when we were together. Such a pretty little girl she was. Always laughing." His fat face grew sad for a moment, then he roused himself and slapping Max on the shoulder, he went into the kitchen. The basement stairs were near the rear door.

"I do not like that man," Mrs. Janik said, sitting back in her red chair. Her friends were sitting around her in a semi-circle, looking like big-busted chickens, while she looked like a frail hungry sparrow. Blinking through thick glasses, she sat hunched and small, her head held away from the fresh doily on the chair's back rest. Mary was a wicked woman, she thought. A bad Catholic. A thousand candles wouldn't shorten her stay in purgatory.

"I do not like that man," she repeated. Her voice was very soft and wispy. Her friends stirred heavily, and made weighty clucking noises as they found new positions for their fleshy legs. Their thick shoes were caked with drying mud.

"He is very big," one of them suggested. The others nodded. Mrs. Janik pursed her lips and blinked slowly.

Stanley had talked of Mary, she remembered. She had insisted on a private room because she wanted to be alone with her husband when he died, and he had talked of Mary. Sitting up in bed once, he had asked her, "Was Mary here, Sophie? I thought she was here and asked me to go for a walk." Mary was dead, a long time dead, she had answered, but he didn't hear her.

He had taken a long time. Three days and part of a third night, and he had talked of Mary, of how she had looked, of how she had laughed. He babbled and smiled about how it had been long ago, living there again and forgetting the old wife he had lived with and was about to leave behind. And all the time in the expensive, private room.

After a while, he slept more deeply, fingers twitching at the edging of the blanket. His mouth wouldn't close. He looked chinless. He breathed through his mouth and it rattled deep in his throat. His chest strained with the work of living.

Sometimes, his breath would catch and the rattle would stop. She would also stop breathing and she would lean forward, a grimace that was the beginning of a wail taking shape on her face. Then his breath would come back quickly and abruptly, the head would turn convulsively from side to side and the throat would swallow.

"Was there something else you forgot to tell about Mary?" she would ask. "Or is it something else that you forgot?"

After a while, she had fallen asleep. Once she had thought that she heard him call a woman's name. It wasn't her name, so she didn't wake.

She hadn't awakened until the light of a misty fall day hurt her eyes. Stanley lay very still and cold. And she began the wailing song of mourning that all Polish women sing for their dead. But her eyes stayed as dry as a child's marbles.

The food was getting cold. Helen went into the kitchen and called the men up. They had been singing Russian songs very loudly. Helen waited at the table. Her husband, Max, came through the door first. He swayed and leaned against the wall, grinning loosely at his wife, his blinking eyes out of phase with one another. She leaned closer to him and hissed in his ear, her eyes slitted with anger. He laughed at her and reached in back to pull his friend, Peter Yaros in the room.

Mrs. Janik suddenly felt very tired. She excused herself and went into her bedroom. She closed the door behind her, but she could still hear the men laughing and talking.

The window that looked out on the street was narrow, and what light came through was dimmed by the heavy lace curtains. But even with her bad eyes, she could see how the flowered red and green wallpaper was coming loose at the corners.

She sat down on the edge of the double bed. It was an old brass bed and it squeaked. They had brought it with them from Pennsylvania. And then, she remembered that the chest standing at the foot of the bed had also come with them. How hard she and her mother had worked—sewing, saving, buying—to fill the chest before the wedding!

Her eyes watered and she got up to get a handkerchief from the dresser. This was another thing that they had brought with them—a tall dark piece with a small mirror fitted to the back. There were two pictures on it. One of Helen and Max and their little girl. The other of Sophie and Stanley Janik taken a few years ago. Stanley had been slight and blond, with a peevish mouth. She thought he had been very handsome as a young man, and she tried to remember, but found that she could only think of him as he had been in the hospital. Cold with sweat, whiskered chin, and the dreams of Mary. "Was she here, Sophie? She wanted to walk by the river. Where did she go?"

She went to the closet, which was on the other side of the dresser, to get a shawl. His slippers were there. They stood pigeon-toed, splattered with paint, toes tilted up. She remembered then that they had forgotten to bring home the new slippers Stanley insisted on getting before going into the hospital. They were red and made of something that looked and felt like leather, but didn't smell like leather. They had been like new, unwrinkled, their soles still white and clean.

It was a sin to be so wasteful, she thought, closing the door and going back to the bed. She sat down.

There was laughter in the other room. She could hear Helen telling Max that he wasn't showing much consideration, and Max telling Helen that he wanted her off his back. And then Peter Yaros started remembering stories of when everyone had been young.

It was always me, Mrs. Janik was thinking, who had to remember that we were poor and getting old. You cannot stay children for always. And growing old is not so bad. Stanley, she sighed, you should have helped me so that growing old would be gentler. But Stanley was always mourning each year and scheming to somehow prove that the dreams and promise of his youth were not all lies.

She lay down on the bed and blinked up at the ceiling. A crack ran down the wall to the hanging crucifix.

How much money had been wasted on his dreams! Like the lathe he had bought so that he could be in business for himself, so that he wouldn't have to worry about lay-offs. And then he learned—after he quit—that he couldn't keep up with the work when the factories were busy, and when they were shut down, he couldn't get any work at all. So he sold the lathe for half what he paid for it. He got drunk on the money and threw both his shoes through the front window. When the factories started up again, they took him back.

She closed her eyes. She felt very old and she still couldn't remember her husband's face. She could still remember his voice, but it had talked of Mary. And she was dead!

"The wedding lasted one week!" Peter Yaros was saying. "From Ohio, four friends of mine come down for the wedding on motorcycles. We play poker the night be-fore—table stakes. I win $1,400, Stanley maybe $200. Oh—they were real mad! And everyone drunk like anything, even Stanley on his wedding night. Even people whose house I live in get a little too much. Only the girl, Mary Ryan stay sober. Never have I seen a woman who could drink like her!

"So Stanley, he leaves, but we keep on with the drinking. And this Mary makes me drink more than I should. And for the first time it happen, I pass out. And when I wake up, you know where I am? Chained to one post of Stanley and Sophie's bed! And you know what is tied to the other post? A pony! Oh, how they laugh on me later. Especially that Mary! Sophie got real mad, but it was just joke."

They had come into their room, she was thinking, seen them in bed together. Stanley said not to be mad, it was a joke, so she slapped him. That was when she started growing old; and that was when she decided that they had to leave that town, and Mary and Peter.

They were laughing in the next room and asking for more stories. Peter whispered because he said he didn't want Mrs. Janik to hear, but she could hear, anyway.

"The time Sophie's father died," he whispered, "everybody stayed up all night with the coffin which is what they used to do. Like always, we had a bottle that this Mary Ryan brought with her. So we sat there in the dark room with the coffin and the candles, drinking, and after while, laughing a little. Mary was always with the men, you know, and the other women didn't like her much. They all went to bed early. Just Mary and three or four other men stay up to drink. One by one, they go out of the room to sleep someplace. Only Stanley and me and one other man—I forget his name—were left with Mary. Then this other man goes to sleep on the floor next to the coffin. So we put a sheet over him and Mary puts candles by the head and the feet. When the other women come down in the morning, how they screamed! Two corpses!"

When she came down, she remembered, Mary and Stanley were sleeping together under the sheet on the sofa. She sat up abruptly, grimacing under the sudden pain of the memory.

"Slut," she whispered fiercely, "slut."

Mary was bad, she thought. A slut who danced and laughed and played with men, and who came to her husband as he lay dying in the expensive, private room. She flinched at the thought and then almost cried out. This was something else that they had brought with them, this dream of Mary Ryan that had lived with them in this house, in this room, in this bed. A bad dream that had lived when only Sophie Janik should have been flesh to her husband.

"What about Mary?" someone asked Peter. "Will she be here today?"

He laughed loudly and gasped. "It would be good if she could, but no. She died just after Sophie and Stanley came to Detroit. They find her by the railroad track. It look like she fell and hit her head. She was very heavy drinker for such a young girl. Only twenty-one, I think."

Mrs. Janik lay back, she pursed her lips tightly, but they started to tremble anyway. Only twenty-one, and Stanley still remembered her and her young laughter. And she would always be young. Coming to her husband at the hospital, she'd come young and pretty and laughing, part of the time in their lives when everything was yet to be.

She pressed her lips tightly to control the trembling, but tears blinded her. Only the dream was flesh. Always. And only Sophie Janik had grown old.

Had she ever been young? She moaned silently, and the bed squeaked with the heave of her sobs.

She was a ghost, emptied of heart. The bed she was lying in was too big, too cold, too empty. From somewhere overhead, she could hear the sputter of a small plane.

Such a Tiny Thing

"T HIS CAN'T BE IT, can it Anna?"

"That's the number from the phone book, Sophie."

Shivering in the crisp, autumn air, the two sisters stopped in front of the house, staring as if it were a freak. They'd had trouble enough finding it, with all the twisted signs and streets bending around water tanks and factories, and under viaducts. It sat on the corner; they'd already walked nearly two blocks from where they parked their car on the last side street, and they were puffing under the strain.

"Lord," Sophie remarked dryly, "a regular doll house. An Honest-to-God little doll house."

Like her sister, Sophie was in her forties. But she was, she knew, the smarter of the two. She stared at the house with the amused tolerance she usually reserved for the antics of children or inferiors, and fingered a tiny gold cross hanging from a delicate chain around her neck. Her younger sister was shorter and heavier, her face filled with the dogged cheerfulness of a long-married woman used to the labor of keeping a factory worker's house and the terrors of slack seasons and layoffs. Unlike the sleek but impractical dress of the elder sibling, which rang with a message of style and class, Anna's modest dress chimed only about how sensible she'd learned to be about clothes.

The house itself was distinguished from the other homes on the block only by its neglect. Peeling, dirty paint, covered its sides, and a narrow strip of lawn in front was overrun by weeds. In back, the wooden fence was broken and unpainted, with weeds and browned stalks of sunflowers poking through the openings. A clothes line ran from the house to the sagging garage, holding a damp night gown drying in the wind. And beside the nearby railroad tracks, looming over the house, was a towering red water tank.

"Oh, this is silly!" Sophie exclaimed at last. "Coming all this way just to stand here."

Staring at the house, Anna saw that someone had drawn aside the curtain slightly and was spying on them from the gloom within. After a brief flurry inside, the curtain fell back into place. "Someone was peeking at us through the window," she whispered, nudging her sister.

"And no wonder," Sophie said sharply. "We must look like perfect fools standing here. Come on. I'm getting cold."

Gingerly, they climbed the shaky stairs leading up to the porch, teetering precariously and holding onto each other for balance. After resting briefly to recover from the exertion, Sophie knocked briskly on the door. After a minute or so, they heard the hurried sound of heavy footsteps retreating deep into the house, a hollow, dark sound that started both sisters shivering, and prompted the younger sister to worry aloud about ghosts. Sophie gave a strained laugh, and was about to chide her sister for being silly, when they heard the door unlatch and both of them jumped with alarm.

A man opened the door. He was a small, tired looking man, with a balding head and meek eyes. He was wearing a heavy blue shirt and work pants, dark with oil. Sophie surmised he'd just gotten home from work because his face was glowing a deep red, doubtless from the scrubbing he'd given it. A small defensive smile was on his lips as he held open the door, and he looked at the two sisters questioningly.

"Does Rose live here?" Sophie asked brightly. The man nodded his head reluctantly.

"Could you tell her that two old friends are here to see her? From back home. Just say Anna and Sophie. She'll know us."

"Yeah, sure, yeah!" the man said, nodding his head vigorously; his voice was thick with an accent. "I go tell her right away. You wait."

He closed the door loudly, and they heard him calling for Rose.

"And it's been nice meeting you, too," Sophie said, bowing to the closed door. "Honestly, now!"

"He just didn't think, Sophie," said Anna.

"That doesn't make me any warmer. Not that we'd be any more comfortable on the inside from the looks of it, but still you just don't leave people standing out on the porch. What kind of man did Rose get herself, anyway?"

She shivered from the cold and hugged herself, frowning disdainfully.

A gang of teenaged boys walked by, shouting to each other as they tossed a football, their words colored by the old country tongue they'd all learned as infants. A breeze tossed some paper and down the street, wrapping itself around a boy's leg as he jumped for the ball. Far off, behind the water tank, a train noisily gathered itself, preparing for the labor of hauling its freight. And the noise of the factories grew louder as the afternoon shift began to pick up speed. The light was becoming uncertain, tentative, and everything was starting to glow with the special, sadness of autumn twilight. The light softened Sophie's rigid, controlled face, making it seem younger, more innocent.

"How long has it been, Anna?" she asked.

"Almost twenty years," Anna sighed.

"Think she'll be changed?"

"Well sure, Sophie."

"I mean much."

"I don't know. Maybe."

"I hope not. I hate it for people to change too much."

Suddenly the man opened the door, and both sisters jumped from fright. He looked painfully ill at ease.

"Rose say she not home," he said, laughing nervously.

"What?"

He looked around, desperately looking for help, before blurting out: "She hiding. Don' wanna come out. I think better you should go."

Loudly, he slammed the door, and the sisters heard his footsteps scurrying away. Stunned, Sophie stared at the closed door, then turned slowly to glare at her sister, who was diverting her eyes and shrugging off any responsibility for what had happened. Shaking her head, Sophie started precariously down the stairs, holding out her hand to call for her younger sister's assistance.

"What on earth!" she demanded.

Safely back on the sidewalk, Sophie turned and looked at the house again while waiting for Anna to catch her breath. Sighing deeply, she motioned for the two of them to begin the trip back to their car.

"I can't understand it," Sophie said, stopping with her back to the house. "Do you think he gave her the wrong names or something? My Lord, I just can't believe that Rose would treat two old friends like that. Especially us. Anna, do you think—?" Suddenly she stopped, aware that Anna not only wasn't listening, but was staring right past her. Turning around, Sophie's eyes widened in horror.

"Jesus-Mary-and-Joseph!" she whispered.

From the clothesline in Rose's backyard, a huge nightgown was making damp, heavy, waves as it dried. Worn paper thin, and torn in spots along the seams, it slapped noisily at the wind.

"So that's why," Sophie gasped, awed by the size of the garment.

"I guess I really can't blame her," she said, regaining her composure, her face resuming its customary brisk and efficient lines. Anna nodded, and they walked down the sidewalk, looking back at the nightgown once more. They said nothing more until they were safely settled in the car and ready to leave.

"Remember?" Anna said softly. "She was such a tiny thing."

Sophie peered at the brown sunflower stalk, nodding and weaving their brittle caricature of summer. Purposefully, she switched on the lights and started the car.

"It was a long time ago," she said crisply.

Sparrows and Ceaves

H E SAT WITH HIS LEGS dangling over one arm of the chair, brooding through the picture window he should have washed the day before. He'd decided, instead, to watch the football game. Now, it was just too wet.

Fall had grown drab, because the rains of October had come back again. The small branches of the young elm tree near the curb glistened darkly from the light cold rain. Two brown leaves had shriveled against the bark, and were now held in place by the wetness. On another branch, two sparrows, swollen against the damp chill, complained bleakly to each other about the weather. The tree stood still under the meaningless rain.

It wasn't even a rain, he moped. It was a mist, an exhaled sigh, the last breath of a decaying earth. It deadened the memory and echo of fall, soaking the land with remorse.

It always rained in October, he mused. Fall always goes out not with a rain but a dribble. He laughed, mocking his weak attempts at being profound.

His wife, who had been washing the breakfast dishes, came to the door between the dining room and the kitchen.

"What was the joke, Al?" she smiled.

"I was just pretending to be brilliant," he replied, quietly.

As she waited patiently for him to share his thoughts with her, down in the basement they heard six-year old Tommy, their youngest son, start building up to a piercing scream that could shatter glass. Meanwhile, Mike—older by three years—was whispering fiercely, desperately trying to reason with his younger brother before the world collapsed around them.

Both parents prepared for the anticipated shock wave, but the blast never came. Good show, thought Al; his oldest son had come through again.

"What was the matter, boys?" Alice called.

"Nothing, Mom," Mike shouted back.

"But Tommy almost screamed. What did he want?"

"Oh, Tommy is playing that silly game again— "

"It is not silly! Not more than your crazy pretend baseball!"

"—and I accidentally knocked it over with a bat. But I told him I'd help him put it up again."

"That was very nice of you. You're being a good older brother." She turned back to her husband.

"Maybe you can talk to Tommy," she suggested. "Not right this minute, but sometime today."

"What's his problem?"

"It's about your father. Seems to be on his mind a lot lately. About how he died, and where he is—now. And what he did and how he sounded. Things like that."

"This game of his, is that part of it?"

"I think so, but go see for yourself."

Two years ago. October, he mused, and a wet day like today. You should forget the dead, the rotting, the things that were. Remember the living, and how the living had been.

A bitter, mocking laugh filled his throat and stayed there like a lump. How profound he could pretend to be, and how safe it was to make believe. But brooding about sorrow was easier than letting it touch him. He could handle sorrow then; study it, dissect it, all the while hiding behind his mask. But handled too much, he thought, it would crumble into nothing, like a dead, brittle leaf.

Al peered out through the picture window. Someone was walking on the road half-hidden by trees in the scrubby field across the street. The man's black raincoat glistened, and his hair was uncovered and silver. A small white dog bounded in and out of the trees, every once in a while wagging its way back to its companion.

A slight ravine beyond the road dropped down to a small creek. Beyond the creek was a small but heavily wooded county park, where the trees were tall and thick. There were narrow paths running along the creek and, sometimes, right down to the edge of sheer two-foot-high cliffs. And dead trees stretched across the creek for adventurous and daring crossings. One summer, Mike and Tommy had exchanged long stares with a raccoon wearing horn-rimmed glasses. For a long time after that, the boys always took their cap guns and toy rifles with them when they went looking for adventure.

In back of the house, everybody's backyard looked into everyone else's. And all the backyards were the same, except maybe better tended than his own. Every yard was fenced, compartmentalized. But the fences were for the adults. Kids knew that fences were for climbing.

When he was a kid, Al recalled, he knew every inch of pavement for blocks around his father's house. Every bump, crack, and tilt—he knew them all like he knew his own body. Then he got older, went to college, to war, back to college; he drank, wrote poetry, fell in love, got married, had kids, got a job. He never saw the sidewalk again; he could never feel that same bump, crack, or tilt. And he never really came back to his father's house.

With a heavy sign, Al decided it was time to talk to his youngest son.

"Don't get upset with him, Al," his wife said as he passed through the kitchen.

IN THE BASEMENT, Mike's baseball cap was pulled low over his eyes. He leaned forward, resting his gloved hand on his left knee, while his right hand nervously played with the tennis ball he was holding behind his back. He shook off two signs from the cement wall. Finally nodding in agreement, he went into the stretch—and then fired and hurled the tennis ball. It skipped off the floor against the wall and bounced right back to him.

"Strike three! You're out!" he called, wiping his head in relief.

"Got him, eh?" his father asked. The boy grinned at him.

"I sure did," Mike winked. "And with the bases loaded and the count three-and-two." Mike was a big boy. His face was open and happy, inviting people to share his joys with him. It was an uncomplicated face, free of disturbing shadows.

Tommy was playing in the secluded space behind a bookcase. He was a thin, intense little boy, with brooding eyes and a beautiful, solemn face. And he was attending a wake.

Tommy had taken a pair of pants and a shirt and some old tennis shoes, and arranged them in an empty caricature of a laid-out corpse. The head was a small beach ball, on which he placed an old, tattered hat. And he was sitting on a chair beside his creation, with bent head and clasped hands.

"How are you doing, Tommy?"

The boy looked up startled, his eyes quickly searching his father's face to see if the question was a friendly one.

"Oh, I'm just pretending this is Grandpa's funeral parlor."

"But why?"

"Oh...I don't know. Just to remember, I guess."

To remember, to understand, to make it manageable so that it can be forgotten. Al stood looking down at the coffin. The pants and shirt were lying flat, just pieces of cloth. But the hat....

"Where did you get that hat?"

"By your work bench. Is it all right?"

He smiled and said it was fine, and rumpled the boy's hair. It was his father's hat and it remembered: looking at it, Al saw it was being worn, cocked jauntily over the beach ball, and he could see the tired, eagle eyes of his father as clearly as he ever could. And he remembered other things he'd saved: scraps of paper with writing on them, gloves that remembered his father's hand, slippers with run down heels, a hammer with the handle worn smooth. He remembered the urgent searches through the closets, the work bench, the desk, when he never knew what the search was for, never knew what he'd found.

"Well now," he said thickly. "Maybe you'd like to take a walk down to the creek?"

"Oh boy, yeah!"

"Me too, Dad!" Mike called. The boys looked up at the basement window; it was beaded with moisture and specked with mud. "It's not raining hardly at all," he added stoutly.

Hardly at all, Al agreed, and he started towards the stairs. "I'll call you in a few minutes," he said, hurrying upstairs.

Alice was waiting with solemn, questioning eyes. He looked at her and felt his mouth twist painfully, searching for his "aren't-kids-the-limit" smile. But there was something wrong with the act, and he could see it in her eyes. And his flip remark strangled in his throat while his expansive arm gesture didn't quite come off, ending in a feeble flip of his hand. They can talk later, he croaked; later. And he hurried to his chair by the window.

All the things collected, Al thought, all the scraps and bits just lying loose, unconnected clues to something. Tommy had his souvenirs, his clues. But Tommy put them together; he made things with them, wringing out the feeling, the sense. Meanwhile, the boy's father just collected and stored and buried them, like some cold, shivering animal preparing for a long winter.

A wet sky rained down onto the earth, sinking deep into the ground. Al saw that the two sparrows had left the small elm, and all the leaves were gone. And so was the old man with his dog.

James Joyce Can Lick
Any Man in the House

AL'S BAR ON WOODWARD AVENUE was long and narrow. There was a row of booths along the wall, and a row of tables between the bar and the booths. The juke box was against the back wall, a cigarette machine was near the front door. The lights were dim, and the dark furniture looked uncomfortable.

A dark man in his mid-thirties, Al kept an unkempt beard and moustache, and wore his sparse black hair cut close. His glasses were thick and dark-rimmed, and his teeth were very bad.

Above the booths, the wallpaper was old and yellow, and looked a little ragged. Al hadn't bothered to change it when he opened the bar because he liked its gay-nineties motif. Lillian Russell was dressed in tights, Diamond Jim Brady was looming over a dish of oysters, and in the center of the wall, squared off against an unseen opponent, was John L. Sullivan. Right beside the Legend of Boxing, a student from the nearby university had scrawled in black crayon the challenge: "James Joyce can lick any man in the house!" Because his clientele was so limited, Al even remembered the kid who'd done it: a skinny little kid with thick glasses. His name was Meyer. He never came back.

"They never come back!" Al complained to one of his few regular customers, Chester Wasilewski, M.A. in English Literature. It was nine o'clock; Chet Wasilewski had been at the bar since five, trying to get drunk and not succeeding.

"And why the hell not?" Al continued querulously. "I stock good draft beer. I keep good stuff on the juke-box. My place is as cramped and dingy with atmosphere as any of the rest of them. And I've got a sexy broad tending bar—"

"Maxine is sexy?" Chet demurred mildly.

"So what the hell, Chet?"

"So Maxine is sexy." Chet shook his head. He and Al were sitting at the far end of the bar, where it curved into the wall. Maxine, the barmaid, was at the other end, near the entrance, talking to a tall, thin man whose head was bent low over a shell of beer. She was a big blond with the face of a boxer. She wore a black turtleneck sweater, and spoke with a heavy, rasping voice.

"Lefty," she was saying to the tall, thin man, "Louis would have cut that bum Liston to ribbons."

"I don't like boxing," Lefty protested weakly.

"Would've busted up his insides and worked him over good."

"I'm a baseball player. Let's talk about baseball."

"And he woulda left a stinkin' pile of blood and crap when he was through." She drew heavily on the cigarette dangling from her lip, blowing a heavy cloud of smoke into the man's face.

"Maybe it's because you're Jewish, Al," Chet suggested to his friend.

"Nine o'clock," Al brooded, "nine o'clock and look at the crowd I got." Besides Chet and Lefty, the only crowd consisted of a very serious young man in one of the booths, deep into a thick book while his coffee grew cold and, in the partially secluded corner booth that Al called his "bridal suite," a whispering, giggling young couple.

Jerking his head toward the couple, Al glared bitterly. "You know why the told me they came here?" he asked Chet. "Because they wanted to be alone. Now I ask you—isn't that a helluva testimonial for a bar?"

Shaking his head unhappily, he called for a shot and a beer. "Bring the same for the Professor," he added.

"I should have listened to my mother. She wanted me to be a rabbi."

"Mothers are always right, Al. Didn't you know that?"

"Yeah, yeah, yeah."

Maxine set the drinks down in front of the two men and waited while they threw down their shots.

"What's with you, Professor?" asked Maxine. "You've been in here all day. No classes today?"

"I called in sick."

She grinned at him. "As they say in the ring," she rasped, "you went into the tank, eh?"

Chet smiled back at her tightly. "You're a very sweet girl," he said, "but mind your own business." She walked away laughing, leaving him brooding over his beer.

The decision had been reached regretfully, the department head had told him, but they could not overlook the fact that he'd done nothing about working toward his doctorate. He'd expected it, Chet told Al afterwards, but it had still come as a shock. At thirty-five, he was finding the life of a transient uncomfortable.

"So what's with this doctorate?" Al asked intensely. "How come you're not doing anything about getting it?"

Chet shrugged off the question, but after Maxine's comment, he began to consider it again.

Originally, he remembered, teaching at the college seemed like the logical thing to do. If you want to be a writer, move into the academic circle, where you earn your living in a climate of ideas, and stimulate your talent—broadening it by studying the great masters of literature. Make the modern novel your specialty. Wrestle with James and Hemingway, Faulkner and Joyce, and force them to give up their secrets. All that was needed was time and energy.

"I'm a baseball player!" Lefty insisted, loudly.

"So how come you ain't playing?" Maxine rasped. "How come you're sitting in here drinking? Is this some new kind of training program?" She laughed coarsely.

"I gave it up," Lefty mumbled. "But just for a while. I'll go back someday and show 'em."

Chet finished his beer. He asked Al to order him another and went into the john. It was an evil-smelling place, lighted by a weak light bulb that turned everything a nauseating yellow. He held his breath as long as he could, but finally laughed out loud when he noticed the pained expression on his face as he washed his hands. Roses can bloom in the crapper, he sighed; don't be an olfactory prude. There's literature here.

When Chet reclaimed his place at the bar he saw two new customers sitting in one of the booths. The two men looked to be in their early forties; one of them stared morosely at the juke box while the other tried to stifle a yawn.

"Customers!" Al whispered gleefully. "Scotch-drinkers, I'll bet. Look at them. Probably haven't been out alone for years, and don't know what to do to raise a little hell. They'd like to go home but they know their wives will needle them about coming home so early. Characters! You know—characters. For some of your stories!"

Al went over for their orders and, winking at Chet, relayed it to Maxine: one scotch and soda, and a bourbon on the rocks. Lefty, at the far end of the bar, waved an empty glass at her as well.

"Take your time, Lefty," she growled. You have lots of it. You're in training, you know, so take it easy."

Time and energy, Chet mused, that's all it would take. Except that time gets filled with other things, and the energy starts to ooze away. And pretty soon, you're thirty-five years old and the drive, the spark has to be rationed, saved for the important things. The important things—that was the rub, he thought. Just what the hell was important: the wrestling matches or the other? The itch or the job?

"I was a first baseman," Lefty said. "The best damn first baseman in the whole White Sox system. Great with the glove, just great. A regular Hal Chase."

"So how come you ain't playing ball?" Maxine asked.

"My weight," Lefty answered.

"Weight?"

"Yeah, I couldn't hit it," he laughed. "And I only weighed one eighty-five."

The juke box was playing a song by Joan Baez: *I Wonder As I Wander*. The couple in the corner booth deserted it as the music started; the boy told Al that it was getting too crowded as he and his girl left. The serious young man with the book slammed it shut, and he left too. Al pointed out that he hadn't finished his coffee, but the young man didn't turn around.

Chet started to feel a little warm, and the room began to shimmer and swim. John L. Sullivan seemed to be striding purposefully towards Lillian Russell. Get her, John, Chet thought, while she's an easy mark.

"'James Joyce can lick any man in the house,'" one of the men in the booth read. He puzzled over it.

"Isn't he the guy who wrote '*Trees?*'" his friend volunteered, and then laughed. "That's a joke, pard'ner. It's from an old Shelly Berman album."

The friend yawned widely. "Let's go to my house and listen to records."

The yawn infected the Shelly Berman fan and he nodded in agreement. "We sure did raise hell, didn't we?" he laughed as they walked out.

Al watched them leave, horrified.

"Two lousy drinks," he wailed. "Two lousy drinks and I lose my crowd!"

"I wonder as I wander," Chet mused, and he thought about that nice old man he'd met long ago. The man had worn a tweed jacket and smoked a pipe, and they met when there seemed to be nothing but time, when the fiber was strong and the reservoir was full. And the man had tried to tell him. You think you're pretty hot, he'd smiled, full of piss and vinegar, and ready to show them all. But sooner or later, he predicted, sooner or later you'll want to go a few rounds with Joyce. Maybe you'll jab him lightly a few times, and decide that this guy's not so tough. And then you'll move in close and he'll grab you and you'll be lost. And you'll find he can find more beauty in a man's shit than you can find in a whole county-full of daffodils. He'll give you a vision of sweat and truth and dedication that'll freeze your spine and turn all that piss and vinegar into foul-smelling slush.

"So I'm holding on the runner on first and Ted Williams comes up to bat. He stands up there like a wet piece of spaghetti, moving that bat back and forth, and he don't look so tough. Two arms, two legs, two eyes, you know? What's so special?"

And you'll die right there, the tweedy man had said, to be reborn an accountant and maybe go on to make a fortune. Or you'll back off and set new goals and write precious little pieces that you'll never sign your real name to.

"This kid pitcher, who's trying hard to make the team, throws bullets at King Ted, and the old man stands down there flatfooted with two strikes on him. He's slowing down, I think to myself. He really is getting old; he can be had. The kid takes his stretch. I give him a target in case he wants to make a throw to first, and he makes his pitch home."

Or you fight him, Chet's advisor had said. You fight him. And the thing that will break your heart will be that he doesn't give a cosmic damn. It'll be like singing songs to a mountain and expecting it to react. All you'll hear will be the echo of your own voice.

"I swear the pitch was by him. I swear it was. I even started to trot in to take the toss from the catcher. Then that bat comes around like a whip, leaning everything into the pitch from his toes up. It was like a cat had learned to swing a bat, and suddenly a white blur comes whistling by my ear. The next thing I know, Williams is standing on second base, and the guy on first is home. And the bastard don't even know what he's done or care about it."

"Lefty," Chet advised, "you gotta forget it. You can't tilt with giants."

"Williams played for the Red Sox," Maxine snickered.

"Two lousy drinks," Al mumbled, "and boom!"

"After the game," Lefty continued, "I asked him how he did it. How did he hit that ball—and pull it down the line yet!—when it was almost by him. And he says, all puzzled like, 'When I see it, I hit it.' Real simple. When I see it I hit it."

"And how'd you do in the game?" Maxine asked wickedly.

Lefty giggled. "I went for broke," he said, "and struck out three times."

Al went around turning off some of the lights, still shaking his head. The traffic on Woodward Avenue was heavy and noisy. Every once in a while, someone's headlight would beam in through the dingy front window and spotlight mighty John L. Sullivan.

Chet wanted to go to sleep; his tongue felt very thick.

"It is simple, Lefty," he mumbled. "If I weren't so sleepy, I'd show you. Very simple."

From the shadows behind the bar, Maxine laughed coarsely.

"You and Lefty, Professor," she chuckled. "Two birds of a feather. It's always going to be next season." Her laughter grew and grew, filling the darkened bar. Even Diamond Jim seemed to be smiling broadly over his heap of oysters.

Selected Poems

Selected Poems

Winter is a Heavy Thing

Winter is a heavy thing
Like too much sleep

The bones ache with Winter
it plays no games—no
Nonsense, please.

Spring is a young harlot
Limpid moist excesses and coy, twinkling
Whispers of green green
Experienced in innocense
The art of pleasing
  A concubine season.

Winter is a heavy thing
yet honest, dependable in its weight, gloom
But honesty isn't something you fall in love with.

I'm Around Here Someplace—

Oftentimes lately, I am lost
And the world becomes an Empty Word
Where nothing sings, where nothing grows.

Such content then—like to a big-lipped
Bruised child—to find your arms.

Consider How It Was

Consider how it was
And how it will be
And
Must.

My father droned heroic poetry from a stage
  when he was young.
He strummed a guitar and sang of Russia
  when he was older.
He trilled a deadly rattle
  when he died.
      Aside from that:
      Was it a nice day? Was it warm?

My wife's uncle Pete squired an American girl
And had his brain knocked loose by some spirited young boys.
He pursued a mother-image and married her.
He drank a hole in his stomach and it was cut out.
  And he raves for pancakes to fill the void.
      Aside from that:
      Is it a nice bed? Are you resting?

My wife's husband wrote poetry when he was younger.
He drank a little when he was older
and watched TV—late.
He practices rattling now.
      Aside from that:
      Are you healthy? Are you wealthy?

The bleak hours come fast
  When a family dies.
Everything that was dies and becomes remembering.
And nothing is to be.

Let the Auto Club—

Never go anywhere in a car.
Take a bus.
But if you have to go anywhere
Get off the pavement.

Look for dirt roads that have been forgotten
   Make the turn where no arrow points
   Where no miles are indicated
   Where no place is reached.

Woods you'll find: quiet, tangled and dark.
   Houses hiding and ponds that don't need your picnics.

And best of all, after a long stretch of close pressing woods,
   Best of all, the explosion of a wide flat sweep of farm field.
And off to one corner, clean and strong against the sky,
   A white silo, a red barn, a gray house with green shutters.

Something Green

I want to write something green
   Something light and fragile as a fat willow's earrings
I want to write something naked green
          Like the first grass pushing up through the brown
             rot of last year
I want to write something green.

Cultural Impotence

Cramped spaces grow clogged
    With must
    Stir with dampness and
    Shadowing rot

Deep, deep holes collect,
    Smelling of old locks,
    Roiling:
                Ancient sea beasts
                Straining over leathery
                Eggs.

Gone

The place is haunted.
  Spook rustling terrorizes the eye corners
And the shadowed steps echo dust through
    twilight corridors
        The paycheck carries nobody's signature...

There were hands that fingered instruments
    coaxing metallic silvery tunes.
  Grease the smell of burn.
And the slap that turned wheels build build.

Where

The light of it
      Curves someplace
In a straight line
      That comes back.

The warmth of it
      The beat of it
Stays there,
      Someplace.

Now

In the absence of knowing
In the lack of becoming
Near the brink of remembering
Near the plunging of predestining
      Is
      A sliver
      Called now.

Given lines and angles
And the cube of creation
Given a formula that moves
And the brassy tickle
Given an itch, a gnaw
Given a flood

The resulting absence
Splits

The Pain of Now

Nothing like the pain of now.
And like the presence of pain makes the nausea on autumn
     hello
The texture of things becomes softer
Then
Shining of gold and yet
Flecked with the echo of green cries
And the benign footfalls of awesome giants
Just below the hill, beyond the horizon, past the season.
    But the time and the pain is now.

Bureaucracy

Everything is Big in the U.S. of A. And getting Bigger...
Except, of course, the people and they're getting smaller.
    Bureaucracy....
      No targets for revolt
      no symbols to loathe
      nothing...
         except Bigness and memos and old golf cards...

I said it first!
Do you hear? I really did
We are the passive generation
The listless, the entertained, the aborbers
  —Sponges—
And history is made behind men's backs.

New Mother

My bride is a little girl.
Sweet pouting mouth.
My bride so soft, so small,
Such large wonder in her eyes.

A big boy, Jeff crawls after her.
Demanding.
Smiling the sweetly selfish smile of babies.
My bride loves him
Works for him
And me.

And she cries, sometimes.
It's hard being bride and little girl all at the same time.

Up North

You ought to go up North.
  Its thick with trees there.
They boil and bubble into round green hills.
They'll explode someday.
      But no one lives there.
      They live someplace else.

You ought to see that bridge up there.
  A clipper ship leaping free.
The human body arched thin and moist with the work of love.
It flies from here to there.

      But no one lives there either.

Well hell, a rose is a rose,
  A smell is a smell.

For Jeff, aged almost three—

Now there are two
where for almost three years you reigned supreme
And the pain of it begins.
   The toys you must share
               Your mother's smiles and kisses
The hurts of occasionally being overlooked.
    Your end as a god.
               Your beginning as a man.
Just remember,
               You were the first to capture our love.
               And its measure will never diminish

Dinner Time

Jeffy jiggles.
Chrissy wiggles.
Mother purses.
Father curses.

   "Eat your string beans while they're hot!"

Chrissy spills.
Jeffy shrills.
Mother moans.
Father groans.

   "The wall's a greasy polygot!"

Jeffy incites.
Chrissy indicts.
Father belches.
Mother squelches.

"Stop that squabbling on the spot!"

Chrissy sulks.
Jeffy skulks.
Mother entreats.
Father bleats.

"No desert unless you squat!"

Jeffy jiggles.
Chrissy wiggles.
Parents done.
Kids have won.

"We'll call when our nerves unknot."

"Have you ever considered," she says to him,
"That you and I are just an interim?"

A Detroit Fog

Morning fog in the city
Makes it small and empty and quiet

Trees along Southfield road
— tired ghosts come a long way.

Jeff

Our Jeff has seen three Summers come and go
   (but only two Falls and Springs)
And he has grown deeply wise and solemn
And intolerant of any adult nonsense
   (it doesn't pay, he says).
Like tonight—
   We were studying a big white moon,
   Jeff and I were,
   From his bedroom window
and watched how it dived (like a fish, he said)
behind the ragged clouds it met
and how it changed the backyard into something else,
something else that we didn't have when we bought the house
      (I asked him, "What?" and he answered, "Something!"
        and I could see that he was right)

Then he jumped
      (I thought, in my grown-up ignorance that he had
      fallen but he said that he had jumped).
And landed sitting on the floor.
   He would jump to the moon, he announced.
To the moon, he repeated getting up.
And I smiled, that I'm-older-than-you smile,
                  and it made Jeff mad.
Sooo—
   :in his blue pajamas that were rolled up because he tripped
   over them sometime:
He scrouched way way down
clenched his fists
made a terrible hard face
and jumped!
And when he landed
he laughed
   Right out loud.

"You see? I told you. Didn't I now?"

I looked around in surprise
and, By George, as always
He was right.

The Brothers

Ed wanted a religion based on four letter words.
    Hate and kill and love and kill and others
    Like a shield in innocent savagery.
    Pick the bones and beat the dreams.
    Dance the dance and grin the grin.
    At the kill, at least one smiles a smile.

Herb wanted a system based on pronouns.
    I and me and us and we.
    We needn't because they might.
    We shouldn't because they can.
    An algebra of ME.
    Preach of love.
    It builds armies.

Rupert wanted a government based on God.
    He had Him picked out.
    Rupert.

Standards and Values

Standards and values
the success of success, the fast buck the new car TV eighty-five dollar
suits
the firm handclasp, the firm chin
the firm steady eye
the laugh the quip the BA
   the right fraternity
   (it wouldn't be fair to the man, really. I don't care myself
   I'm just thinking of him)
the right neighborhood the right wife the right nurse
Nurse
   All right: like you say
   It's all for the birds, oaty and hot roasting on the pavement
   and if you look hard enough you'll always find it.
If you forget about looking, even
That's the trouble really how it is
   you forget just looking
   do this like me maybe:
   Find: A Tree,
     A glancing light,
faraway figures,
     deep stretching night
   Find: A Face, haunted,
    Eyes,
      an open window
A shadowed door and muffled voices: something
to step through and close and lock
   something to fling open and someplace
to run for running and to fall for falling.
It's all very well to say: protest
It's all very well to protest: this is what it should be and not that
It's all very well to say that: things are unbeautiful, unkind, unjointed.
But let it be someone else

I saw a tree today
  slim and red and dying all alone
  and the air dusty and sharp with the rumour of Winter
and I saw that tree

That's why I can't say: protest like
Only: me
Looking for anger and targets for scorn blinds the eye
Blinds the heart
But only: me
  And maybe me can well and often
  And maybe hold and give.

Dying

  Got that new Ford today.
    Smooth,
  Exciting feel over bumps
  Jet smooth quiet
  And trees flowing into one another.

  Then a squirrel under the wheels
  Smooth
  No bump, no sound.
  In the mirror he lay still
  Then jerked alive
  Long bushy tail lashing
  Struggling to the curb
  To die.

  Christ! What a crazy damn
  Squirrel.

The Block

If there's a was
there must be a been
which means there could be a be

Once, remember, living song
the eyes read poems too fast for hand to hold
  Rain hanging, full-bellied from green
  Budding April spilling miniature Niles
  In the mud and the wondrous deltas at the edge

  Of porous sidewalks
  The splash of it was like the diamonds of cymbals
  The spark of water

  Even later with Autumn
  The faraway straight smoke
  Long hellos from woods steeped in gold and reverence
  Shaking off leaves like dogs:
  Melody coming then fading too quicky
    When you forget

  Even later
  With the hard cosmetic of Winter
  And haloed street lamps
  The fog of breathing

All these made dumb the world
Needed puzzling furrows
And poses and words that trembled and lit fires

It's 10:30 and tomorrow
Spring must be met
Or Winter comes to be seen again
And stays too long.

The Chameleon is a Small Lizard

I am a chameleon
  Would you talk of politics?
    Look no further! Satisfaction guaranteed or your money
        back!
Perhaps religion?
  Say Mac! Try the ten-day plan! Return me, no questions
  asked, no obligation.
  Baseball, football, golf?
  Compare with what you've been using and you'll switch!
  The Arts?
  Before you decide, see me!
Sex?
  Friends, you owe it to yourself!
Perversions of Sex?
  No money down! No payments!
Gossip? Racial dirt? Petty hates? The movies?
  It's Here! It's Me!
I am a chameleon.
I accept the terms laid down.
I submit. I need friends.
I've lost the need for principles
  Or dogma, or values.
I am a chameleon.

Don't Tell Me About Poems, Jack!

We can see Summer turning to go from our front window
Dust biting into the weeds across the road
Patches of sky showing where before it had been solid green
   And the haze and smoke of Autumn hangs heavy on the open
fields
   as I leave for work
Every year at this time I listen carefully
   Because some one always calls to me from faraway
   Most of the time I only hear the trailing end of the cry
    the mourning bluenote that finishes
   Somewhere in the smokey haze and dust and rustling harvest of
    leaves someone is reminding me of something I'd forgotten
Every year at this time I hear it
But:
   Not as near as before
At least:
   Nearer than afterward.

Poems don't just spill out
   Beautiful, complete like seven poplars on the crest of a hill.
They come hard, coyly uncooperative
   Like a nail that persists in missing the hammer:
It would be better to have done with them.

Don't worry, they said, you'll outgrow it.
Well...
   I'm still waiting
   I've outgrown quite a bit:
    My baseball shoes, bubblegum,
    The Rover boys, movies
     (Not cowboys)
    And the pleasures of drink (too much)—

But this other thing:
   I read a line of something and it strikes tender and hollow:
   reverberations and echoes:
   And I'm a stranger
Or walking, I look into a face
   Or watch a bird fly
   Or study a stupid puppy sitting in a puddle of water
Most it seems to be red trees, big-bellied and alone
If I could avoid red trees I think I'd be all right

It's about the middle of September
When the red trees come—
—Damn red-headed trees—
The year sighs a long, shuddering sigh
and, all of a sudden, whoosh!
There they are—
—These damn red trees,
Fat, round red trees
   standing like fatlegged little kids,
Quiet
   not asking you to notice
   but hoping you will:
"Do you like me this way?"
"Do you think I look pretty?"

Yes, dammit, yes!
Only leave me alone
I don't want to write poems.

Tomorrow's Monday

Sundays die with starts
Of neon flickers, where a breeze
Ruffles a street lamp's shadows.
  Paper
And rope and a roto section
And boys study magazines
In a slow drugstore.
  The traffic light
Repeats itself time and again,
Like the absent prayers of the troubled.
Dust and dust blow through.
  It's the time
Of the thief in the market aisles,
Time of the cat in the emptied lot,
Time of the siren in some other place.
  Across still ball fields,
Under lullaby trees,
Windows cry light,
Antenna fingers sift the air.
  Heels ring sinister,
Glowing cigarettes ominous.
Dogs pass the word from yard to yard:
A walker! A walker!
  Down the grass nibbled pavement,
Under the face brushing fingers
Of old, old trees that little boys leap for.
  Sundays should also die profoundly:
only the very young know
the exciting crack and buckle of sidewalk.

The Man Died

Look at his shoes
  See how they...
Maybe his gloves
  The way they...
Perhaps his hat
  How it...
Or his house and the furniture
  The way it...

It all fit so well, and still remembers.

What's up?
  poking in closets
    pulling out drawers
  turning scraps of paper

What is it, in the garage?
  behind it
    Under the peach tree
  beneath the shrubs

This flexed work glove on the basement stair?
  What?
This glove retains the habit of a hand:
This son searches like a boy,
  lost, lost.

September 8, 1957

Dear Jeff and Chris:
  I want to talk about your grandpa again.
  You will forget him soon.
     And you should.
  Your concern is and should be with living
  not with death. Death will come in its own good time.

  I will forget him too.
Not his face: pictures can always bring it back.
     but what he was and how he was in the round.
  I will forget:
     how he sat, how he turned and walked,
     how he spoke, how he laughed;
     the smell, sweat, flesh of him will never come back.

  In this letter, I'm hoping to save something of what he
was so that when you read it later (when you learn how) you will
know a little of him,
     and when I read it, I will remember.

He was a remarkable man, my father.
His age was an age of remarkable men.
Just think of this:
     he and millions like him left their native
land and came to this strange new country to do something. To want
to do something is like being hungry sometimes.
     And trying to do something, they did something.
Starting with as much of nothing as you can have and still be
alive, they made monuments of their lives.

  So he was a remarkable man, but he never believed it.
Just as Columbus or Washington or Galileo never believed
they were remarkable men.

When they thought of themselves, they
thought of themselves as men, growing old and soft, with families
and responsibilities they hadn't particularly sought,
     and saddled with opportunities that
they'd missed,
     and saddled with the sense that somewhere
along the way their lives had taken a turn they
hadn't counted on.
     But fumbling along, tripping, slipping,
Complaining—like my father—they marked and named their years
And changed, maybe a little bit, what they found when they came.

     But my father always thought of himself as a failure.
His life wasn't complete,
   Its end was ragged.
          Everyone's is:
you don't get a chance to dot all the i's and cross all the t's;
Death always comes before you've had time to finish tying your shoe.
     Come to think of it, everyone fails. It's part of the curse
of being a man.
     I'm wandering.
     About my father now—

What he looked like, you can tell from the pictures in the albums
your mother keeps. You can tell from them about the shape of his
face, how his eyes looked at you, how round and short he was.
     But you couldn't tell how dark he was, how rough his cheek
and chin.
     when I was little like you, he used to rub his cheek
against mine to make me squeal and giggle because it felt just like
sandpaper.
     You couldn't tell how big his head was for such a short man.
And with his hairline gone, how his broad rounded forehead made
it
look even bigger.

You couldn't see much of his profile: the high forehead, the
fine nose, the sensitive delicately drawn lips.
             I can remember when
I was a little boy, maybe 7 or 8, adoring my father's profile.
We were driving somewhere, my sister and mother were in the
back seat of the model A Ford, my father and I were up front.
And I couldn't take my eyes off my father, his face etched sharp
against
the sky.
   I studied him for along time. Remembering now, I think
what I learned from that study was that there was a proud man, a
fierce angry man, an explosive man.
             He never took his eyes off the
road, never showed by any sign that he was aware of my study.
But thinking back, I think he must have known how closely and
adoringly I studied him.
             And it must have made him happy.

I guess I'm telling more of how I loved him than of him, but it's
harder than I thought.
He loved his native Russia.
The older he got, the closer to Death, the more he loved it.
You can understand that.
He played there, learned there.
H ran and felt there.
He left his mother there (he never knew when she died).
He buried his father there when he was still a little boy.
He saw his oldest brother killed there
(he and his brother were digging at a hill of rock salt that had
frozen solid through the winter and it collapsed on top
of the brother, and he was dead).

He loved his native Russia.
Everything that had been happy and young,
Strong and full of hope had happened there.

If he'd lived in a different time,
if the country hadn't been racked by a depression when he was young
with a wife and family to worry about.
If.
   It's hard for a man to be noble and strong and proud
when he doesn't know whether he can feed his family.
And then, it kills something in a man when he knows he can't and
has to ask for help.
   Try to imagine how a strong proud man must feel
to have to sit in a kitchen watching his wife doing her housework,
while he sits staring out the window doing nothing because
something's happened to the factory whistles.
What does he do with his rage?
With his pride?
With his hope?

   Sure, other people went through the same thing.
   Sure they did.
But I'm not talking about other people, but my father.
Maybe he was a poet like your father would like to be.
Poets can't live with Economic Truths.

   My father never recovered from the depression.
He lost the young sense that he had control over his destiny.
For the first time, he faced the prospect that things outside
could destroy him.
       And something in him that was young and vital
and full of sunrises died.
       And turned into something else
that was old and sour and dark.
That's the way it will always be.
   Men build an image of themselves:
   Everything must fit that image.
   Then one day, there comes a second,
   or a minute,
       or a day that resists the shaping.
   And the image shatters.

What you are then, depends on what you do with
the pieces.
With my father, your grandfather,
the pieces stayed underfoot until the day he died.

But for me and I hope for you, this:
   A powerful, strong dark brooding man whose angry love
manifested itself in the sweat and effort of his work.
The eye, fierce and hawklike.
The rough touch and rage that was sweeter than the softest hand,
   the softest whisper.
The sevenfoot tall of him.
The courage of him when Death presented its card.
His faith in his beliefs and principles.
   — whether right or wrong—his faith.
   He was a man.
      I was lucky to have him for a father.
I hope (but doubt) that you'll be as lucky.

         All my love, Jeff and Chris.

John: 11:22:63

Once upon a long time ago (maybe yesterday)
      there was a brief shining moment that made the world young.
The moment passed a long time ago (maybe yesterday)
      and the world grew bitter with age.

Yesterday (or maybe a long time ago) a new moment sparkled briefly,
      a promise flashed like a quick smile and then was quenched.

And the world grows old and cold and too sad for bitterness.

An Ode to Exxon and Lost Children

A while ago (maybe yesterday) I saw a
Squirrel commit suicide
It was sitting at the side of the road...
Every once in a while it would alert up on
  it's haunches, front paws pressed together in prayer.
Leaning out to look down the road....

      This was a while ago (maybe yesterday)
When the TV screens were filled with
      —Black slick long-beaked birds trying
         to flutter out of black slick water and dying
      —Otters with simpering silly smiles
         blinking in embarrassment because they
         couldn't do what otters do
      —Acres of floating fish, seals.
It was the season of nausea

After a while (maybe yesterday) a car came down the road.
The squirrel waited, reached in prayer, until the car
     was a wheel turn away
Then it ran under the front wheel.
There was a red spat
     The tail twitching, then a fur accent on the pavement

And maybe a while ago (yesterday)
There were pictures of little ones
     wearing chains in urine-soaked beds.
And faces blemished by blue and red
     streaked swells and young eyes staring
     big and puzzled filled with "why?"
And somewhere else fly stricken eyes and
     mouths of surrendering bones, staring, losing the will to ask
"Why?"

Getting Old

Lonely is an aged word
If you are loved and loving, you are not alone
The young may agonize over their isolation,
    But they are stealing the sense
    of the widowed, the wifeless.
If you recognize that each day we live is a gift,
    That the now is the ultimate.
    That the now is the end.
    That the now is the now
Then the touch, the act, the gesture
    is an act of love
    and the act of love
    is the ultimate expression of now.

The question of death comes up...
  Now and then
Usually in rooms cloyed with the scent of arrangements,
The tinge of relief, the touch of regret.
Sometimes...
    it comes with the touch of winter, the twinge of autumn,
    the cry of spring
But most coldly...
    It comes alone
      In a room when the beat of time is strongest
      When the purpose is shadowed...
As long as there is no reason for its coming
It is not noticed,
But that's why the question keeps coming up.

Being Eighty-Five

I'm eighty-five, you know
That's old, you know
Everything seems used, seems in need of repair
You know
The future is getting shorter,
    The days shorter
Friends become pensive
    Alert for sighs, pains
        You know
The only lightness that comes, you know
Is the squeal of a two-year old's laugh.

ABOUT THE AUTHOR

WALLACE CAMINSKY was born in 1922, the first-born son of immigrant parents. After struggling through the Depression and World War II, where he served in the South Pacific, he finished college in 1947, graduating with a degree in English from Wayne State University, and was married the following year, soon to start a family of his own. Working for one of the Big Three automotive companies in Detroit, he wrote intermittently for the next twenty years, before embarking on a second career as a lawyer. He went to law school in the 1960s, and became an administrative law judge in 1975, serving in that position until his retirement in 1987. Always a voracious reader, his tastes in literature range from the short stories of James Joyce and P.G. Wodehouse to the novels of Charles Dickens, and the epic classics of Tolstoy...as well as the comedy of Monty Python.

www.ingramcontent.com/pod-product-compliance
Lightning Source LLC
Chambersburg PA
CBHW020838260626
47169CB00003B/1037